MURDER
ON THE
MOUNTAIN

CAROLYN LAROCHE

----------HOT TREE PUBLISHING----------

Murder on the Mountain © 2020 by Carolyn LaRoche

For information, contact the publisher, Hot Tree Publishing.

WWW.HOTTREEPUBLISHING.COM

EDITING: HOT TREE EDITING

COVER DESIGNER: BOOKSMITH DESIGN

FORMATTING: RMGRAPHX

E-BOOK: 978-1-922359-05-6

PAPERBACK: 978-1-922359-06-3

For my boys.
You inspire me to be
a better person every single day.

CHAPTER 1

Emma tripped over yet another root and whacked her face on a low-hanging branch, the bare wood dragging across her cheek and catching in her hair.

"Ahh!" The tangled mess yanked her head back until the branch snapped and momentum sent her stumbling forward.

"Ouch!" Grabbing on to a small boulder, she saved herself from a total face plant in the dirt. Her hands slipped on the rock, tearing a layer of moss off it and scraping her left palm. Emma wiped the green and red mess off on her jeans. "Gross."

So much for stealth. Anyone else on the mountain had probably heard her coming four roots ago.

Her cheek felt wet. Emma touched it with her fingertips and inspected the red moisture. More blood. "Well, that's gonna leave a mark."

Wiping her hand on her jeans once more, next to the moss and mud stains, she continued trudging up the mountain to the serenade of crickets and croaking toads.

The afternoon had already begun to slip away. If her source was right, an abandoned hunting cabin should sit nestled against the rocky mountain face about a five-minute walk from her current position. Emma pulled out her cell phone and checked the location against her present coordinates. Yup. She just had to follow the rough path a little bit further.

The way the sun had dropped below the tree tops told her it'd be dark by the time she headed back to her car. She'd tripped on roots in the light; hopefully her guardian angel would be on double duty to prevent her from breaking her neck on the way back down the slope. She needed to see that cabin though; it could be the link she'd been missing in her story.

"You're definitely earning that pizza for dinner right now, girl." Emma swiped at the sweat on her forehead with the sleeve of her fleece jacket and pushed forward until the path took a sharp turn to the right. Another hundred feet or so, and she entered a small clearing complete with the hunting cabin she'd been looking for. Bending at the waist, she took a few deep breaths to satisfy her oxygen-starved lungs.

The cabin sat in the middle of the clearing. Overgrown grass and brush filled the space between the trees and the cabin, browned and crisp this late in the fall. This side of the cabin showed no sign of human inhabitants.

Weathered wood and a rusty tin roof that had definitely seen better days made up the structure in front of her. A sagging front porch that barely looked attached wrapped around from the front to the only visible window.

The sun glinted off the hood of a shiny black sedan with darkly tinted windows that sat in the partially hidden driveway. It would have been nice if her source had mentioned she could *drive* up the mountain.

Of course, he'd also told her that no one would be here.

Emma pulled out her phone and hit the record function. "The cabin is small. One room, maybe two judging from the outside. Looks like there is only one way in. A black Lexus is parked out front, windows tinted too dark to see inside. Note to self, if I were a movie director, I'd definitely use this place for a B-grade serial killer movie. Also, another note to self, hiking a mountain is no longer on my bucket list. Not that it ever really was."

Dusk had begun to settle over the mountain. Glancing from the cabin to the car, she debated her next move—leave undetected or risk being seen by whoever was in the cabin. The car in front of the cabin could belong to anyone. She'd bet real money, though, that it was no one she wanted to meet alone in the almost dark woods. Maybe just a quick look inside and then she'd get out of there. Emma tucked her phone in the inside pocket of her fleece and crossed the small space to the cabin, taking extra care to be extremely quiet. When she reached the building, she moved to the side of the window and peeked in through a tiny opening in the ragged curtains, sucking in a breath.

A man stood in the center of the small room, the gun in his hand pressed against the temple of another man. The second man was tied to a chair and had a piece of shiny silver tape over his mouth.

The man with the gun said something and then pulled the trigger. A loud bang filled the air, and the man in the chair slumped forward.

Emma clapped a hand over her mouth to stifle the scream that tried to escape. The shooter looked toward the window. Had he heard her? She turned to run, her boots instead slipping on some leaves, sending her crashing to the ground.

Heavy footsteps moved across the floor of the cabin, echoing in the quiet woods around her.

Emma scrambled to her feet and ran for all she was worth, crashing through the brush, no longer even trying to be quiet.

The door to the cabin slammed open as she sprinted for the pathway back down the mountain to her car. The air reverberated with the echo of several gunshots. Tiny hairs prickled on the back of her neck as a light whistling noise passed her ear.

"Stop! I'm warning you! Stop or I'll shoot you!" The man's voice echoed off the trees but she kept running. It was a stupid thing to say, since he had already tried to shoot her. Her gut told her there was no way she'd get out of this alive if she stopped moving.

Halfway down the mountain, Emma's toe caught one of those roots again. The action sent her sprawling to the ground, and she began to roll down the mountain. Grabbing at branches and brush, she finally stopped herself and pulled her aching body up off the ground. Her knee burned where the fabric had torn and flesh had scraped against the ground.

Footsteps and voices sounded behind her, but they were further away than she'd expected. Her little fall seemed to have given her an advantage. She pulled herself up, ignoring the pain in her injured knee, and ran as fast as she could.

The sun had almost completely become lost below the treetops; the darkness made it hard for her to navigate. Finally, Emma burst out of the trees, gasping for air and sweating like a fiend. Her old car sat quietly, right where she'd left it. She dug in her pocket for the keys, but they were gone.

She must have lost them on the way down! Running straight to the back of the car, Emma groped around up under the bumper. Her fingers grasped the small magnetic box and she pulled the hidden key out of its safe storage container, grateful her father had insisted on putting it there when she left for college. As she ran to the driver-side door, the back door window exploded beside her, covering her in tiny little pieces of glass.

Yanking open the driver door, she jumped into the seat, slammed the door shut, and jammed the key into the ignition. Just as the engine turned over and she floored the gas pedal, the man from the cabin ran out of the woods. Her tires ground into the shoulder, spewing a cloud of rocks and dirt. Eventually, she gained control of her car and took off down the mountain roadway known as the Blue Ridge Parkway. Clutching the wheel, she prayed she'd stay on the road.

All the way back to Staunton, she kept an eye on the rearview mirror. When a dark-colored car came into view, she panicked, but it had a different shape than the one she'd seen and turned off a couple of exits later. As soon as Emma hit the Main Street exit, she drove straight through town.

Twelve years she'd stayed away from Staunton, avoiding her hometown and missing her parents, to not have to do the very thing she was about to do. Emma took a deep breath and steered her car onto the street that housed the Staunton Police Department. She had no other choice. There was only one man who could help her figure this out.

She parked in front of the station, ignoring all the little pieces of glass that rained off her as she ran up the steps and pulled open the heavy front door. The entire station fell silent as she strode to the front desk, leaving a trail of leaves and little bits of broken glass behind her.

"I need to see Detective Adam Marshall. It's an emergency." She looked around the lobby. "I don't even know what time it is. Is he even here?"

"He's still here." The officer behind the desk reached for the phone. "What happened, miss? Do you need a medic?"

"No! I'm fine. I mean, I'm not, but I am. Can you just get Detective Marshall for me, please?"

He set the phone back on the receiver. "Just wait right here and I'll get him."

"Don't worry." Emma crossed her arms over her chest. "I'm not going anywhere."

* * *

"Sir?"

Adam looked up at the sound of the voice and tap on his

office door. "What's up, Murphy?"

"There is a—woman—at the desk demanding to see you. She says it's an emergency."

Adam narrowed his eyes at the young uniformed officer. The other man had a tendency toward the dramatic, but he'd proven himself in the field. At the moment, he looked really concerned. "Are you not sure if she is a woman?"

Officer Murphy shook his head. "It's not that. You, um, have to see for yourself."

"Okay." Adam pushed his chair back from his desk and stood up. "Show me what you got."

Adam followed him out to the lobby desk but froze when he saw the woman standing there. Sticks and leaves tangled in her shoulder-length brown waves. Dirt and dried blood smudged her face, a tear in her jeans bared a scraped knee, and her light blue fleece jacket had a variety of colorful stains on it. He hadn't seen her in so long he might not have recognized her under all the debris, except he'd know that woman anywhere.

"Emma." He walked a little closer. "What happened?" What he really wanted to ask was *What are you doing here?*

"We need to talk." She glanced around at all the people staring at them. "In private." Emma leaned in a little, lowering her voice, as though it would matter. "It's about a crime."

He motioned toward the way he'd come. "We can talk in my office." To Murphy he said, "Please get Ms. Thomas a bottle of water."

"Yes, sir." Officer Murphy disappeared in the direction

of the break room, and Adam led Emma to his office.

When they were inside and the door was closed, Emma collapsed into one of the chairs, shaking. Tears ran down her face, leaving streaks in the dirt as they trailed to her chin and dropped onto the front of her jacket.

Adam perched awkwardly on the edge of his desk, a box of tissues extended to her. Emma grabbed a couple and wiped at her eyes, then blew her nose.

"I'm sorry. I'm so not a crier." She threw the tissues in the trash can. Her hands shook noticeably.

He remembered that about her. "It's the adrenaline dump. Nothing to apologize for." A knock sounded on the door. "Come in!" Adam called.

Officer Murphy walked in and handed the bottle of water to Emma. "Do you need anything else, miss?"

She shook her head, and Adam gave him a nod of dismissal.

"So, are you going to tell me what happened?" Adam finally asked. *And maybe why you specifically asked for me out of all the cops in this precinct.*

Emma nodded and wrung her hands in her lap. "Yes. I just—I need a minute to gather my thoughts."

"How did you know I'd even be here?"

She shrugged. "I didn't. I just hoped you would be."

Adam walked over to the window and looked down at the street. A silver sedan, with a missing back window sat under the streetlamp. The light caused the inside of the car to sparkle, and suddenly Emma's appearance made a little more sense.

"Emma? Did someone shoot at your car?"

She looked up at him, relief now mixing with the fear in her hazel eyes. "Six years as an investigative reporter and no one has ever fired at gun at me. Until today."

"Do you know who it was?" Adam moved back over to where Emma sat, pulling the chair beside her around so he could sit and face her. "Emma? Do you?"

"I was looking into some—a tip for my newest exposé, and I saw a man shoot another man. I slipped and fell when I tried to run away. The shooter heard and chased me down the mountain. Just as I reached my car, he fired one last time."

He listened as the words tumbled from her. Emma had witnessed a murder. He knew what that felt like. Ignoring the image of Leslie's limp body lying on the floor of her apartment as well as the longing to wrap his arms around her and hold her close until the shaking stopped caught him off guard. "Do you have any idea who these men were?"

Emma shook her head. "There wasn't supposed to be anyone at the cabin. I'd heard it was just a drop spot."

"A drop for what?" Adam asked, praying she wasn't talking about what he thought she might be.

Emma sighed. "I've been doing a series of stories on the supposed drug issues here in Staunton. You know, while I house-sit for my parents. I want to expose the people involved and put an end to the trafficking."

Adam narrowed his eyes. "That has never been confirmed."

"Please, Adam. I am not a fool. I do my job as well as

you do yours." Annoyance flashed in her eyes, highlighting the gold flecks scattered through the green irises.

He gave himself a mental shake, forcing a long-ago memory to go back to where he'd hidden it for over a decade. "Where did you go today?"

"A source told me about an abandoned hunting cabin just off the Blue Ridge Parkway. He thought it was a drop spot for the supposed traffickers. I just went up there looking for some drugs to take pictures of. You know, evidence. After I wrote my story, I planned to email you the details of the location. I didn't know I'd stumble on a murder."

Her voice shook a little, tugging at Adam's heartstrings. It had been so long since he'd gotten to look at Emma, hear her voice—he had made a conscious effort to avoid her since that night all those years ago. Even on social media, he skipped past any mention of her. But now, as she sat there looking so shaken and determined all at once, he found himself torn between throwing her out of his office and grabbing her up in a hug.

"Adam? Are you listening to me? I saw a man get murdered."

Her frustration tugged his focus back to where it needed to be. "Yes, I heard you. I'm just trying to make sense of it all. You went up the mountain, on a hunch, to find a cabin that may or may not be part of a drug trafficking ring and witnessed a murder."

"Yes!" she said, jumping up and pacing. "He killed that man. And I have no idea why."

"Did you know the man?"

She shook her head. "Nope. I don't have a clue who it was. Just some bad guy, I guess."

"Are you sure he is dead?"

Emma glared at him. "Of course I'm sure! Are you going after the guy or not?"

"It's a little more complicated than that. I don't even know where you were."

"I can show you." She grabbed his hand and tried to pull him toward the door.

Adam pulled his hand free, holding it up in a sign of surrender. "Whoa! Hold on there, Emma. I can't let you go back there."

"Why not?" she demanded. A fire grew in her eyes that had a funny effect on his insides.

"Well, because someone just tried to kill you. And, if a murder did take place there, then it's also a crime scene."

"So, what do we do now?" she asked.

"We're going to sit down, and you are going to tell me what you know. Once I have your full statement, I'll get a team together and go investigate."

"If we don't go now, he'll get away."

Adam rubbed the light scruff that had shown up on his chin since that morning. "I'm pretty sure he left the moment you got away. So, tell me what you know so I can get to work."

Emma narrowed her eyes at him. "Fine. But before we do any of that, I need the ladies' room. My hands and face are filthy."

She definitely was a mess. Adorably so. Pushing those

thoughts out of his head, Adam pointed to the door. "Take a right and follow the hallway until you see the sign for the ladies' room. I'll be right here when you're done."

Emma disappeared through the door. Adam sat in his chair and steepled his hands in front of him. Looking up at the ceiling, he said, "Lord, grant me plenty of strength to get through this night. I'm going to need it."

Picking up his phone, he dialed his boss's number. If he had a murder investigation, then he needed the crime scene unit and some backup ready to go.

CHAPTER 2

"Oh, wow."

Emma froze when she saw herself in the mirror. As if the foliage in her hair wasn't enough, little bits of broken glass adhered to the fleece of the jacket, shimmering in the fluorescent light. Unzipping it slowly, she slipped one arm out, then the second, and folded the whole thing into itself in an effort to avoid sending bits of broken window all over the bathroom floor. Setting the wadded-up jacket in one of the sinks, she turned on the taps in the sink in front of her and waited for the water to warm up.

Seeing Adam for the first time in so long hit her like a kick in the gut. The way he'd looked at her when he saw her in the lobby—it was like twelve years hadn't passed since they last saw each other. But it had, and it had been good to Adam. Really good. His athletic teenage frame had filled out into a strong, muscular form that oozed power and strength. The youthful intensity still lingered in his eyes, with a shadow of something else. Something darker. He was her high school friend Adam Marshall all grown up, and oh, what a man he had become.

Squirting a good amount of soap into her hands, she stuck them under the water and lathered up. The first time she saw Adam Marshall in more than a dozen years and she looked like she went three rounds with a wrestler in a compost pile.

Maybe it hadn't been the best idea to run to Adam for help. She'd done such a good job of avoiding him all these years that she'd almost lost track of the heavy-duty emotions she'd packed away so long ago. Now he knew she'd come back to town and all those emotions were trying to announce themselves again.

Scrubbing at the smudges and scrapes on her face, she tried to ignore the images of Miranda in her wrecked car. Images she'd filed away in the never-to-look-at-again box in a deep, dark recess of her brain.

Emma leaned down and rinsed her face with the warm water. Rivers of mud ran into the sink and slid down the drain, like the mud that had run across the road during a nor'easter all those years ago. Straightening, she grabbed some of the standard, scratchy brown paper towels and patted her skin dry, closing her eyes against the images of blood and twisted metal.

"At least you look like a human now," she said to her reflection. "Sort of, anyway."

A sharp rap on the door made her jump. "Be right out!"

She picked another twig out of her hair, then smoothed it down as much as she could. Without a hairbrush and a clip, she couldn't do much more. Taking a deep breath, she pulled the bathroom door open and stepped out into the hall.

Adam leaned against the opposite wall, arms folded over his chest. "I nearly sent someone in to check on you."

"I brought half the mountain in here with me. Took a minute to get rid of it. Wait, I forgot something." Emma went back into the bathroom and grabbed her jacket from the sink, then returned to where Adam waited. "Do you happen to have a bag I can put this in?"

Adam nodded and motioned for her to follow him. Right before they reached his office, he pulled open a supply closet and grabbed a rolled-up plastic bag. "Here. Best I can do."

Emma accepted the bag, shaking it open with one hand. The word *Evidence* was printed on the front in big red letters. "Does this mean you're confiscating my jacket?"

He laughed, and she caught a glimpse of young Adam once more as his eyes twinkled with mirth. "Do I need to?"

"Nope." Emma opened the bag and slipped her jacket inside. "This works perfectly. Thank you."

"Let's go talk." Adam led the way to his office while Emma tried to ignore the fact that she had once kissed him and suddenly would very much like to do so again.

When they were settled in his office with the door closed, Adam leaned back in his chair and crossed his arms. "So, tell me the entire story. From the beginning."

Emma grinned. "I was born on a very cold day in February—"

Adam raised an eyebrow. "You know that's not the beginning I meant. Who told you about the cabin?"

"I'm a reporter, Adam. You know I'm not going to give

up my source. I don't have to."

He nodded. "Okay, then. Tell me where it is."

Emma pulled a crumpled piece of paper from her back pocket and handed it to him. She'd already snapped a photograph of it earlier in the day, so if he kept it, it wouldn't matter. "These are the directions my source provided." She pointed to a spot on the sketched map. "This is about two miles south on the Parkway right past the rest area, on the left side."

Adam nodded and made a note on a sticky notepad on his desk. "What did you do once you got there?"

"I parked my car and followed the path to the clearing where the cabin is. Like I said, I just wanted to get a peek inside. Maybe snap a few photos."

"Were you looking for anything in particular?"

"Drugs."

"Did you expect to just see a big pile of cocaine or marijuana sitting in the center of the floor?"

She frowned. "Of course not. But I didn't think there'd be a murderer there either."

Adam leaned forward, his expression serious. "You could have gotten hurt. Or worse, been killed."

Emma stood up and threw her hands on her hips. "I'm not a fool! I wasn't going to go rushing in there and try to save the day. I just needed some evidence that the cabin is the drop spot my source named it as."

He sat back in his chair again. "Well, at the very least, you were interfering with a police investigation. I'm sure you did your research and knew that the drug issue has been a multiagency concern for several months."

Emma sat back down. "I didn't touch anything or talk to anyone. It's not like I planned to witness a murder."

Adam nodded, slowly. "I know. What can you tell me about the gunman?"

Emma shrugged. "There wasn't a lot of light so the details are hazy. He was tall and slender with long, dark hair tied back in a ponytail. Oh, and he wore a suit. Something dark."

"And what about the victim?"

"All I saw was his profile. He wore a ball cap, so I couldn't even tell you what color his hair was."

"How do you know it was a man?"

Emma narrowed her eyes at him. "Um, I don't know. I guess I just assumed."

Adam made another note on the sticky pad. "So, you have absolutely no idea who either of the men were? You're not protecting anyone?"

She shook her head, her eyes narrowed at him. "I didn't stick around to ask for names. Once the killer knew I was there, I took off running as fast as I could."

"When did your car window get hit?"

"I guess when I was getting in it. The guy chased me down the mountain, firing his gun a few times. All I could think about was getting out of there though, so I don't know how close he got or how many times he fired."

Adam nodded. "I suspect you've just gotten mixed up in the local cartel. They're going to be looking for you. Any chance they know who you are?"

Emma shrugged. "I'm not sure how they would."

Adam stood up and walked around his desk, leaning against it with his arms crossed over his chest. "This source of yours, can you trust them?"

She crossed her arms over her chest. "I'd like to think so."

"My question now would be, why? Why did they send you up that mountain? To get your story, or to stop you from writing the story—permanently."

Emma hadn't thought about that. When the anonymous email had come, she'd thought maybe she'd been asking the right people the right questions. She'd been so excited to get the hand-drawn map it never occurred to her it could be some sort of setup.

"What's wrong?" Adam asked, looking concerned.

"Nothing. Why?"

Adam frowned. "You've never been very good at lying. What aren't you telling me?"

Emma jumped up from the chair, positioning herself so that she was practically eye to eye with the man she'd tried so hard to get over. "It's been years since we've even talked to each other. How do you know I'm not an excellent liar? I could be into all sorts of underhanded things now and you'd never know because you don't actually know me anymore."

* * *

Emma stared at him, the set to her shoulders and the fire in her eyes igniting a different kind of fire inside him. What she said had merit. It had been over twelve years since the last time they'd seen each other. There had to be plenty he didn't know about her.

Just like there was plenty she didn't know about him. How would Emma react if she knew he'd basically been responsible for his girlfriend's murder not even three years ago?

That didn't stop him from wanting to pull her close. The desire to hold her in his arms grew greater with every passing second.

He pushed all thoughts of Leslie back into the lock box he'd erected in his brain and focused entirely on the woman in front of him. "I'm sorry. You're right. But I still think there's something you aren't telling me, and that comes from ten years of being a cop, not your former best friend."

Her cheeks colored slightly. "Okay, fine. It's possible it could have been a setup."

Adam narrowed his eyes and frowned. "A setup? By whom?"

Emma shrugged. "Someone who doesn't want me to write the story."

"What makes you think it could have been a setup?" Adam asked.

She let out a long breath of air and relaxed against the seat back, almost as though she was resigning herself to the fact that she had no choice but to tell him everything. For her own safety.

Adam watched her and waited as Emma picked at a thread in a hole in her jeans. She worked the thread with her fingers until it came loose. Finally, she looked up and spoke.

"I received an anonymous email a few days ago. It said they knew what I'd been looking into and that someone would be in touch with very important information that would help me make my case."

"Did that happen?" he asked.

"I expected another email. Instead, I got that map, delivered to me while I was having lunch at Pop's Diner. I didn't recognize the young man but he knew exactly who I was."

"Who here knows why you're in town?"

She shrugged. "I didn't think anyone other than my aunt and uncle did. Every person in Richmond I've told thinks I'm housesitting for my parents while they are away for a few months." She glanced toward the window. "Which reminds me, I've got to get home. The dogs have to be fed and walked."

"It's only a little after seven."

Emma stood up and grabbed the evidence bag with her jacket in it. "They get mean when they're hungry." She laughed. "Who'd have thought a four-pound ball of fluff could be anything but adorable."

He didn't like the idea of her going home alone but knew he couldn't stop her either. They didn't have that kind of relationship anymore. Pulling a business card out of the drawer in his desk, he handed it to her. "This has all my contact information. If you remember anything else or need anything, don't hesitate to call me."

Emma accepted the card and tucked it into her jeans pocket. "I don't need a babysitter though."

Adam frowned. "I'm not a babysitter. You're a witness to a murder, and I don't like the idea that someone might know that."

"For a moment there, I thought you were about to say don't leave town."

He smiled and gave her a wink. "I figured you weren't going anywhere since you've got the dogs to worry about, but yeah, don't leave town."

Even though she was turning away, Adam saw Emma roll her eyes. A little reminder of the old Emma. Good, she was still in there. Maybe he'd get the chance to see what else about her had stayed the same.

No. His friendship with Emma had ended that night all those years ago. This was strictly work. He had too many hours invested in the trafficking investigation. If Emma had stumbled onto a key place or player, he needed to know. And protect her as a witness.

Yes, as a witness. Not as the beautiful, green-eyed woman of his childhood dreams.

Adam walked over and opened his office door. "Like I said, call if you need anything. I'll head up there at first light and see what I can find out."

Emma nodded. "Yeah. Okay, and thanks." She patted the pocket where she'd tucked his card.

She walked away before he could say anything else.

Suddenly, his life had just gotten a whole lot more complicated.

CHAPTER 3

Adam stood by his window and looked out as Emma exited the police department and walked to her car. The pieces of broken glass in the back seat twinkled like tiny stars under the streetlights. Emma being shot at worried him. It meant the killer considered her a loose end and he would probably try to tie it up as quickly as he could. With any luck, the shooter hadn't gotten a good look at her license plate.

He watched as she left the parking lot and drove away from the station. When her taillights finally disappeared around the corner, he grabbed his extra flashlight, the little map Emma had given him, and his car keys, then walked out of his office.

"You heading home?" Higgins, the desk sergeant asked as he passed by.

"Not yet. I've gotta go check out a possible shooting on the Parkway."

Higgins looked confused. "I didn't hear anything go out over the radio."

"The woman who just left? She reported it." Adam

tapped the radio on his hip. "Shooter is probably gone. I'll call in for backup if I need it."

Higgins made a note on a pad. "Okay. Be safe out there."

Adam nodded and left the station.

Opting to take his own truck rather than his patrol unit, he headed out in the direction of the Blue Ridge Parkway. He knew the little pull-over spot that Emma had talked about, and he'd spent his teens and early twenties hiking all over these mountains, so he knew the terrain like the back of his hand. He even thought he knew the cabin she'd been to. He and his buddies used to hang out there when they got too cold on hunting trips. Getting there would be easy, even in the dark. The only thing that really worried him was what he'd find inside the cabin once he got there.

Red-and-blue flashing lights met him at the entrance ramp to the highway. A state police car blocked the ramp, and the officer standing in front of it approached him.

"Ramp's closed for another ten minutes or so," the trooper said, walking up to Adam's open window.

"What happened?" Adam asked.

"Rig rolled over. Wrecker is pulling it out now." The trooper lifted his light and peered in at Adam. "Marshall! I thought you sounded familiar!"

"Hey, Chang, how's it going? How's the wife and kids?" Randal Chang had been in every class Adam had ever taken from kindergarten through graduation.

Randal nodded. "All great, thanks for asking. How 'bout you, man? Adam Marshall take the leap yet?" Randal clapped a hand to his mouth. "Oh, man, I'm sorry. I didn't

23

mean—Leslie—Oh, crap."

Adam raised a hand, stopping his old pal's apologies, and shook his head. "Nah, man. Married to the job. That's about all I can handle right now."

Randal shifted his weight, resting his hands on the sides of his duty belt. "I really am sorry about your girl. You hear Emma Thomas is back in town?"

Adam shrugged at the sharp turn in conversation from one heart break in his life to the other. "Yeah."

"You okay?" Randal asked.

"Why wouldn't I be?"

He shrugged. "Just wondering." Randal clapped him on the arm. "It's been a long time, man. Looks like the wrecker's pulling out, so I'm gonna move my car. Stay safe out there, buddy."

"Yeah, you too." Adam gave a little salute and rolled up his window while Randal jogged back to his cruiser and slid in behind the wheel.

As soon as the road reopened, Adam continued his journey. The parkway was quiet and dark most of the way. A few sets of taillights in the distance, and one set of headlights behind him, and that was it. He saw the rest area Emma had mentioned up ahead and decided to park his truck there. The pull-over spot was only a few hundred feet past it, and he felt better leaving his truck out of sight after what had happened to Emma's car.

Parking as close to the exit as he safely could, Adam locked his truck and tucked one flashlight in the pocket of his jacket. The other he held in his hand as he walked, sweeping the area in front of him with light. When he reached the spot where Emma had been parked, he could see very clear tire tracks in the dirt. With his cell phone, he took a quick picture, then another of a footprint nearby. Pushing into the brush, he found the hiking trail that the map indicated and started the climb to the cabin. He looked up at the evening sky. A million stars sparkled above his head.

Somewhere in the distance an owl hooted. Night insects sang, and a gentle breeze stirred the branches over his head, making an eerie clacking sound. Late fall meant the forest inhabitants would be prepping for the cold winter that sat just around the corner. In a few weeks, bare branches would catch ice and snow, making it a true winter wonderland. The mountains were the only reason he hadn't left Staunton after high school. He couldn't bear to be away from the only home he'd ever known.

Much clearer than he'd expected, the trail was easy to navigate using Emma's little map. After about fifteen minutes of trekking uphill, he broke through the trees to a clearing. The temperature had dropped several degrees, so he could see his breath in front of him as he viewed the tiny cabin in the center of the clearing.

A branch cracked behind him. Adam spun, his gun in his hand, just in time to see a possum scurry away. Turning off his flashlight but holding on to his gun, he slowly walked along the edge of the clearing, surveying the building from all sides. No cars or any other signs of life. Advancing slowly, he peered into the first window he came upon. The interior was dark. He moved to the next window and then the front door. He pulled a glove out of his pocket and put it on. Standing off to the side, he reached over and turned the knob slowly, inching the door open.

When no one tried to shoot him, he slipped inside the cabin, leaving the door open for a quick getaway.

Turning his flashlight on again, he made a quick sweep of the space with the beam of light. In the center of the room, a wood chair lay on its side next to a dark stain on the floor. Striding closer, he knelt down and lit up the stain. It had the dark red color of blood starting to dry but the unmistakable coppery scent was what convinced him. He snapped a couple more photos with his cell phone. Straightening, he slowly flashed the beam of light in a wide arc around him. A tiny glint under the edge of a cabinet caught his eye.

Adam walked over to the piece of furniture. Leaning down, he snapped a picture of the item before he picked up the shiny piece of metal between two fingers. Just as he'd suspected, it was a bullet casing. Looked like a .45 caliber cartridge. Emma's shooter liked big guns.

Working the glove down his wrist so it came off inside out, he made a makeshift evidence bag to hold the casing in. He stowed the whole thing in the inside pocket of his jacket.

A loud scream echoed outside the cabin, causing him to drop his flashlight with an equally loud crash. Scooping up the light, he shut it off and ran outside. The sound of sticks breaking and dried leaves crunching filled the night air. Adam ran toward the sound, certain it had been Emma's voice he heard and worried what he'd find if he caught up with her.

* * *

Emma tripped over yet another root and landed on the soft dirt, her face burying in some rotting leaves. Jumping up and spitting out the organic matter that had gotten in her mouth, she kept running, ignoring the dirt in her eyes.

Footsteps sounded in the forest behind her. Emma sprinted as fast as she could, but she could hear her pursuer getting closer.

Why hadn't she listened to Adam and just gone home?

Because she needed this story. If she didn't break something big, and soon, she might as well consider her childhood bedroom home, permanently.

As she rounded a bend in the path, someone grabbed her shoulder. Emma screamed and tried to get away, but strong arms wrapped around her from behind, a hand covering her mouth.

"Emma! It's me!" Adam's voice sounded next to her ear, his hand moving from her mouth.

"Adam?" She spun on him, anger replacing fear. "What are you doing here?"

He put both hands on her shoulders, holding her in place. "I could ask you the same. I thought you were going home? You know, where it's safe."

"I was. And then I made a detour. I still need to get my story." She rested her hands on her hips, trying to look annoyed. Hopefully Adam couldn't hear her heart pounding in her chest, because that sucker was working overtime trying to clear the adrenaline spike she'd just had. "Why'd you have to go and chase me down the mountain?"

Adam shook his head. "I didn't chase you until you screamed and ran. I thought you were in danger."

She shrugged. "I thought I was too. That deer had huge antlers."

"You were afraid of a deer?"

"He was big and looked hungry."

"Deer don't eat people. Even the big ones. They like grass and leaves."

"Whatever." She gave him an annoyed look. "You still didn't have to grab me like that. You could have just told me who you were."

"I didn't know if we were alone out here. I was trying to keep you quiet."

Emma narrowed her eyes at him. "By making me think I'm being kidnapped?"

Adam made a slow circle. "We are alone out here, aren't we?"

"That depends. Were you the one in the cabin with a flashlight?"

Adam nodded. "Yes. I found some things that corroborate your statement."

"You mean you didn't believe me? You had to corroborate it?"

He sighed. "I'm a cop, Emma. It's my job to find evidence. I investigate crimes. You reported a crime. I know you understand this since you are an *investigative* reporter."

"I witnessed a crime and I told you about it. Eyewitness testimony is very powerful." She had no idea why she was arguing this with him when she really just wanted him to wrap his arms around her again and make her feel safe. Now that she knew it had been him and not some bloodthirsty hit man.

"But solid, physical evidence holds up in court." He held a finger to his lips and dropped his voice to a whisper. "Shhh. Did you hear that?"

Emma shook her head.

"A car door just slammed shut down the mountain." Adam started moving slowly through the brush. "Stay here."

Emma ignored him. "No. That's my car down there, and besides, I have had enough of thinking someone is trying to kill me out here in the dark."

"Fine. But stay close." He led the way back to the base of the mountain where her car sat.

With his gun raised, Adam scanned the area before stepping out of the cover of the woods. Emma followed him.

"Looks like there was another vehicle here." Adam pointed to some fresh tracks beside her vehicle.

"Yeah. I'd say so. Look." Emma pointed to her windshield where a white piece of paper tucked under the wiper shifted in the slight breeze. She walked over to her car and reached for the paper but stopped when Adam placed a hand on her shoulder.

"Wait! Don't touch that." He pulled out the second glove he had in his pocket and used it to pick up the paper by its corner.

WE KNOW WHERE YOU LIVE. BACK OFF. NO POLICE AND WE WILL FORGET YOU EXIST.

The letters were printed in large, block script.

Emma felt the blood drain from her face. Her knees went a little weak, and she clutched Adam's arm for support. "How do they know? It's not like I introduced myself after the shooting."

"It could be a bluff. Maybe he came back to clean up the mess I found in the cabin, saw your car, and recognized it. Decided to scare you off a little."

"It says no police. Did I sign my own death warrant by going to you for help?"

Adam shook his head. "I don't think so. Cartel hit men aren't in the habit of leaving loose ends. They won't stop until they find you. If it's not a bluff, then it's a blatant warning they are coming for you and want it to be as easy as possible. I don't think you should go home tonight."

Emma leaned against her car and sighed. "Where do you suggest I go? I still have my parents' dogs to take care of."

"Since it's going to be nearly impossible for you to find a place that you can take the dogs tonight, how about I go home with you?"

"I don't think that's a good idea, Adam." The thought of him hanging out in her parents' house just like when they were kids caused a little flutter in her chest.

He raised his hands in front of him in mock surrender. "In a purely professional capacity. I'll be your bodyguard until we can arrange some kind of protective detail or something."

She looked at him, a hundred unspoken questions passing between them. "Do you actually think I'm in that kind of danger?"

He nodded. "I think you could be. Until I know what really happened up there on that mountain and who is responsible, I need to know you're safe. I couldn't handle it if something happened to you too."

He meant like Miranda. She could see it in the shadow of sadness that passed over his expression. After so many years, he still carried the guilt of their friend's death. Emma slumped against her car. "I don't want to die."

"So I'll stay with you tonight, and in the morning we will see about boarding the dogs so you can stay at a hotel."

She nodded. "Fine. What choice do I have? If you really think I'm in danger, then okay. I need to run to the store on the way home, so meet me there in about an hour?"

"I'll take you. We can leave your car at the station."

"But I'll need it in the morning."

"I'll bring you back there to get it. I have to work tomorrow, so I'll have to go there anyway." He smiled at Emma but she didn't smile back.

"Okay, fine." She still thought it might be a bad idea to be that close to Adam for so long. They had so many things between them that had been left unresolved for so long. "Only because I really am worried they might come looking for me."

A little ding indicated an incoming text message on Emma's phone. She felt Adam watching her as she opened the message. Her body swayed slightly as she whispered, "No."

He grabbed for her as her knees buckled, lowering her to

the ground slowly. "What is it, Emma?"

She handed him her phone as she collapsed against his chest. "Someone wants to know if I got their note. If they have my cell phone number, then they really must know who I am and could even know where I am staying."

Emma trembled in Adam's arms. He rubbed her back lightly and spoke low against her ear. "I'm not going to let anyone hurt you. I promise."

She nodded into his shoulder. She knew he meant the words even if there was no way he could keep that promise. She stepped back and swiped at her eyes with the sleeve of the hooded sweatshirt she wore. "I'm sorry. I'm not usually such a baby. I'm sure it's just a scare tactic. I've been threatened before. In my line of work, I ask questions. Questions people sometimes don't like to answer. I should expect to make some people angry."

Adam gently lifted her chin with his finger so she had to look at him. "This is not the same, Emma. Don't you get that? You witnessed a murder. They know who you are."

"It's not like I wanted to."

"I know that. But you did. And now someone wants you dead." Adam stood up, pulling Emma to her feet as well. "We need to get out of here. Whoever it is could be watching us right now."

His expression remained guarded, but Adam's eyes had always been the window to his soul, and she could see the worry for her safety churning there. Emma nodded. "You're probably right. This day just needs to end."

"I'll follow you to the station. We'll lock your car in the

back lot."

"Okay." She got into her car without another word and drove away.

CHAPTER 4

Once they parked Emma's car in the gated lot behind the station, Adam took Emma back to his office to log the bullet casing and the note from Emma's windshield into evidence and download the photos he'd taken to his computer. Emma had sent him a screenshot of the text message and the phone number it had come from, so he downloaded those as well. In the morning, he'd get a tech guy in the lab to try and trace the number. Finally, he called the lieutenant, who had already gone home for the night, and updated him. They agreed to hold off on the crime scene team until morning. It would be too treacherous in the dark and dangerous if the shooter returned.

When he hung up the call he'd arranged to put a marked car near the rest area and another at the base of the long road that ran up the other side of the mountain to deter any further activity.

"You ready to head out?" Adam asked Emma as he logged off the network.

"I guess." She sat by the window, staring out into the

dark. "You really don't have to go with me. I don't want to keep you from your family."

Adam shook his head slowly. "You're not keeping me from anyone."

Emma stood up, hugging herself. "Won't your wife be worried?"

He walked over and pulled the door open. He couldn't bring himself to say out loud that he'd become a lonely bachelor, so he shrugged. "I'm not married. It's not an issue."

She followed him, silent questions in her eyes that he wasn't ready to answer. Did she know about what happened in the years since she'd left Staunton?

When they reached his truck, she didn't wait for him to open the door like he'd intended. She just climbed into the passenger seat, closed the door, and put on her seat belt. The drive to the supermarket passed quickly—and quietly. Emma looked out the window, basically ignoring him. When he pulled into the lot and parked his truck in front of the store, Emma opened the door and jumped out almost before the vehicle stopped moving. He turned the vehicle off and climbed out as well.

Emma raised an eyebrow at him. "You don't need to come with me. I'm pretty sure I can handle this on my own."

He nodded. "I'm sure you can. But if you don't mind, I need to grab a couple of things too."

"Fine," she replied, walking ahead of him. "I hope you don't embarrass easily though. I need some feminine hygiene stuff."

"I think I'll be fine. Go get what you need and I'll meet you at the registers." Adam watched as she entered the store, shoulders set and stride quick. He didn't really need anything; he had a completely stocked go bag in his truck. He hadn't eaten much that day though, so he figured he'd grab a few supplies, maybe cook them something to eat at the Thomas house. What he really needed to do was keep Emma in his sight as much as possible until they could get the whole murder on the mountain thing sorted and ensure her safety.

No way would he stand by and let someone he cared about die when he had the ability to protect them.

Someone he cared about.

Funny how Emma had been out of his life for a dozen or so years, yet the moment she'd walked into his station it felt like no time at all had passed.

"Are you coming?" Emma stood by the automatic doors, watching him.

"Yeah. Just keeping an eye on things." Something felt wrong. He scanned the semidark parking area but saw nothing amiss. Still, he let his hand rest on the gun on his hip. Better to be ready if something went down.

They entered the store together, but Emma immediately walked away from him, saying, "I'll meet you at the register when I'm done."

He didn't want to make her uncomfortable by following her around but it made him nervous having her out of his sight. The little hairs on the back of his neck tingled, giving him an unsettled feeling. Hanging out in the produce department near the entrance, he grabbed a couple apples, a bunch of bananas, and an avocado. The dairy section adjoined the produce department, so he picked up a dozen eggs and some sharp cheddar cheese, never once letting the front door out of his sight. As he browsed the Greek yogurts, a man wearing a dark suit and sporting a long ponytail entered the store.

Adam pushed his cart toward the front of the store but quickly lost sight of the man. Leaving his groceries behind, Adam strode toward the first aisle and looked. Nothing. He checked two more before a man wearing a manager's tag stopped him.

"Can I help you find something, sir?"

Adam held a finger to his lips and showed him the badge clipped to his belt. "I'm looking for a man in a dark suit with long hair," he whispered.

The manager pointed to aisle seven, his expression losing its friendliness. "He went down there," he whispered back. "Please don't shoot up my store."

That was the least of Adam's worries. "Get your employees off the registers and all of you get in the cash office. Lock the door and don't open it until I tell you."

The manager nodded and jogged away, waving to the cashiers as he passed by to follow him.

"Adam!" Emma's frightened voice filled the store, followed by a shot. And then a second. The sound of breaking glass sounded as Adam sprinted in the direction of the gunshots.

"I know you're in here!" a voice he didn't recognize

called out. "Come out, come out, wherever you are."

Adam rounded the corner of aisle seven and saw the man standing at the end, his back to him.

"Police! Drop the gun!"

Slowly, the man turned and made eye contact with Adam, his gun still in his hand.

"Drop the gun on the floor!" Adam yelled.

"I think not," the man replied. Raising his weapon, he fired two shots. Adam jumped behind a display of canned soup as both bullets flew past him, a little too close for his comfort.

Adam leaned out from his hiding place and fired two shots of his own. The man disappeared. Adam bolted down the aisle after him. When he reached the end, he caught sight of the shooter's long hair as he ducked around another corner.

"Emma! Stay where you are! I'll be back!" he yelled, praying to God she wasn't lying on the floor somewhere bleeding. Or, worse, dead.

Sprinting, Adam made it to where the shooter had been but the aisle was empty.

"He ran out the front door!" a voice said over the loudspeaker. "We saw him run out!"

Adam ran to the door and out into the night just in time to see a dark-colored sedan speed out of the lot. Spinning in a slow circle, he scanned the area but saw no one else.

Emma.

Holstering his gun, he turned and sprinted back into the store. The manager and his employees were leaving the office as he passed the customer service counter, but he didn't stop to check on them. He had to find Emma.

"We're fine!" the manager yelled after him. "Thanks for asking! Not that I can say the same for my store."

Adam didn't stop to respond. All he could focus on was Emma.

He ran to the back corner of the store and looked around but saw no sign of her.

"Emma! He's gone. Where are you?"

"Adam." He heard his name and spun toward a pile of packages of toilet paper just in time to see a pack slide out of the way, exposing Emma. "I'm right here."

He pushed the toilet paper aside, clearing a path. "Are you okay? Did you get hit?"

She shook her head. "I'm fine. Just a little shaken up."

Adam reached up and tucked a piece of hair behind Emma's ear, then ran his thumb over a smudge on her cheek. "You've got a little something—"

Before he could finish his sentence, Emma launched herself into his arms. "He tried to kill me, Adam! Again."

He smoothed her hair, letting his hand run lightly down her back. "I know, honey. I'm so sorry." Emma's body trembled as he held her. He pressed a kiss to the top of her hair. "It's all right now. I've got you."

"I've been in some sticky situations before but this is the first time someone actually tried to kill me. Now, twice in one day." Emma stepped back. "I don't know what's wrong with me. I can't stop shaking."

"Just let it happen. It will pass in a few minutes. It's

the adrenaline." He took her hand and led her toward the front of the store. "Let's get you home. I want to feed the dogs, then get you somewhere safe."

She shook her head and stopped walking. "What about the house? And the dogs?"

"I'll get a patrol car to check on it through the night."

He could see she had started to waver. "I can't just leave the dogs there. Do you know a hotel in town that will let me bring them?"

Adam took a deep, steadying breath. "I'm sure we can find a place."

Emma pulled her hand from his. "I want to go home tonight. I'll leave in the morning. I need my laptop and my clothes and—"

Adam ran his hand through his hair. "I don't get you, Emma. You're the one that showed up at the police department asking for help. I'm trying to help you and you resist me at every pass."

"I went to the station to tell you about the murder. Not because I wanted you to put me under lock and key." Emma stormed off, marching toward the front doors with her shoulders set and her back straight. When she got there, she stopped walking. Crossing her arms over her chest, she leaned against the wall and stared out through the glass.

Her back-and-forth emotions were just a response to what had happened. Textbook behavior. But it didn't stop the frustration from welling up. One minute she wanted his help, the next she was pretty much telling him to take his help and shove it. Adam strode after her but stopped when he remembered the store's crew. "Y'all okay?"

"Yes," a young girl answered. "Thank you so much for saving us."

"Do you know what that was all about?" the manager demanded.

"Not really," Adam answered, walking toward the door. "I'll call it in, though, and get some uniformed officers over here. Please don't touch anything."

As he approached the doors, he could hear the sounds of Emma crying quietly. She didn't even turn to acknowledge him, just followed him to the doors.

Gun in hand, Adam stepped through the sliding doors and stopped, surveying the lot.

Emma stayed behind him. He couldn't tell if it was to keep him from seeing her tears or because she wanted to use him as protection. Either way he'd take it.

"Looks okay but stay behind me anyway until we get to the truck." Adam glanced back at her. Emma nodded but didn't say anything. He half expected her to bolt across the lot. She didn't leave though, so once they were inside the truck, he pulled out his phone and called the desk sergeant. As soon as he was certain officers and the crime scene people were on the way, he ended the call and put his phone back in his pocket.

"Let's go. I feel like sitting ducks out here like this." Adam reached for her hand, but Emma tucked it in her pocket.

As they headed toward the lot exit, two police cruisers pulled into the lot with their blue lights on. Adam opened his window and waved them over.

One of the cars pulled in close and opened a window as well. "Hey, Detective. Heard you got shot at buying toothpaste or something. That explains a lot."

Adam shook his head at the younger officer. "Very funny, Jones."

"Seriously, though. Any idea who the shooter was or where he was headed?" Officer Jones asked, glancing around the parking lot.

"He took off about three minutes ago in a dark-colored sedan. I didn't catch the tags so there's no BOLO. Right now, I just need y'all to go inside and make a report. Take a few statements and document everything for the insurance claims they'll have to make. Crime scene on the way?"

"Yeah. Glad you two are okay." Jones pointed toward Emma. "You need one of us to take her home?"

"Thanks. I'll get her where she needs to be. You guys just get this place processed, please."

"Will do." Jones pulled his car away, the other car following him to the fire lane in front of the store.

* * *

"Let's get you home now." Adam put his truck in gear and headed out of the parking lot.

Emma turned away from the passenger window to look at him. "You're still going to let me go home?"

"You've got to take care of the dogs. It's nearly ten o'clock as it is. I'll stay on the sofa and keep an eye on things. You get some sleep, and in the morning we will figure out a plan."

Emma nodded slightly. "Okay."

They made the drive to Emma's parents' home about a mile outside the city in silence. Emma stared out the window, trying to ignore the fact that her heart still beat hard and fast in her chest and her hands still trembled slightly.

At one point, Adam fiddled with the radio. After flipping through every single channel twice, he finally settled on a local station known for playing an eclectic mix of past hits. An old rock ballad came on, something she'd listened to plenty of times in her life but one particular memory of a Christmas party long ago filled her mind. Emma stole a glance at Adam, wondering if he remembered also.

He made no move to change the channel, but he had a white-knuckled grip on his steering wheel.

For the first time in a really long time, Emma let the memories of that night play through. The youth group party with all of their friends had always been the highlight of the holiday season. Emma and Miranda had gone all out, getting their nails done, fixing their hair, and buying new dresses. Miranda couldn't wait for Adam, her most recent crush, to see her all dressed up. Unfortunately, it hadn't been Miranda that Adam looked for that night.

The kiss had been tiny, a little peck really, but they'd been under a sprig of mistletoe and their friends had cheered them on until Adam finally leaned in.

"You smell nice," he'd whispered when he'd kissed her. "And you look beautiful."

Emma would never, ever forget the look on Miranda's

face as she walked into the room carrying two sodas just as their lips made contact.

"You're remembering too, aren't you?" Adam's voice interrupted her trip down memory lane.

"I never forgot," Emma replied, not looking at him.

"I haven't either," Adam replied. "If it weren't for me, she'd still be alive."

"You don't get to shoulder all the blame there. I was her best friend. I knew how big her crush on you was. She felt betrayed."

"I know," Adam said quietly. "It was supposed to be a harmless kiss under the mistletoe."

Emma studied her hands, picking at some loose nail polish. "If only she hadn't run out of there. If only she'd let me explain."

Adam reached over and squeezed her hand lightly. "If only she'd let us explain."

Emma looked at their entwined fingers. "I don't know. Maybe it wouldn't have helped. That kiss didn't feel so harmless to me, and Miranda could always read me like a book."

They reached the end of the drive leading to Emma's parents' house. Adam pulled in and stopped the truck. Turning, he looked at her, his eyes searching deep into her soul. "If I could change that night, losing Miranda that way, I would. I'd have run faster, stopped her from getting in her car, or chased after her and stopped her before she could wreck. But the one thing I would never go back and change would be that very sweet, much too brief kiss under the mistletoe with you. I wish we'd done things differently."

"Me too. So many things. Adam—" A single tear escaped the corner of her right eye and slid a slow path down her cheek. He reached up and smoothed it away with his thumb, the light contact setting her heart to race mode once again.

"Shh... I know. I miss her too. And I have carried a lifetime of regret with me since that night. Regret that Miranda saw us and regret that she died. But I don't regret kissing you. Not one bit, and the day may come where I'd like to do it again, no mistletoe needed."

He turned back to the wheel, set the truck in gear, and continued on down the rocky path that led to the house. Emma wanted to say something, fire back some sassy remark that took the seriousness out of Adam's comment, but she had nothing. Pretty much because she felt the exact same way. No man she'd kissed since that night had affected her the same way, and it had been the standard to which she'd held all her dates. Unintentionally... or maybe completely intentionally.

CHAPTER 5

When they pulled up in front of the house, Emma could
see the dogs in the front window barking at Adam's truck.
Grabbing her purse, Emma jumped down and headed
toward the front door, keys in hand.

"Wait!" Adam called after her. "Please. Let me go in
first."

"Why?" Emma asked.

"Because I have the gun." Adam pulled his gun from the
holster and held it out in front of him.

She rolled her eyes but stopped and let him go first. After
the day she'd already had, she had no interest in any more
surprises.

They followed the light-lined path to the front porch.
Adam paused at the foot of the steps and looked around
them slowly. Then, one step at a time, he cautiously made
his way to the wide wraparound porch. Emma said a silent
prayer of thanks that she'd thought to leave the light on
inside that morning.

They could hear the frantic tapping of little dog paws on

the other side of the door. The matched set of terriers her mom had rescued a couple of years ago scampered back and forth on the tile of the foyer, yapping and barking.

"How many dogs?" Adam asked her.

Emma held up two fingers. "Just two. Brother and sister. Mom named them Lucy and Ricky."

Adam nodded. "That's it? Sounds like a dog army on the other side of this door. Can I have your key?"

Emma handed him the front door key. Adam inserted it into the lock and turned. The lock didn't click.

"Are you sure you locked the door this morning?" Adam whispered to her.

Emma nodded. "I sure hope I did. Dad would have my hide if I didn't. Retired cop, remember?"

"Then we might have a problem. Stay behind me, okay?" Adam didn't wait for her to respond. He pushed the door open slowly and stepped inside.

The alarm system chirped, letting her know she had thirty seconds to punch in the code. At least they knew no one had been in the house. Maybe she really did forget to check the lock that morning.

Emma waited in the foyer as Adam moved from room to room, checking windows and looking behind closed doors. He cleared the entire ranch-style home before he spoke.

"Looks all clear to me. I'm going to run back out to my truck before you set the alarm."

Emma nodded. "Okay. I'm going to check the kitchen and see what I can find for dinner. You hungry?"

"I could eat."

Emma dropped her purse on the table in the living room. "I'm going to let the dogs out first."

"Okay," Adam replied, walking toward the front door.

After sending the dogs out the back door to the fenced-in yard and a quick trip to the powder room where she washed her hands and face, Emma headed to the kitchen.

When she got there, she found Adam standing in front of the refrigerator. "Your parents sure keep a nicely stocked fridge." He grabbed some eggs, sausage, an onion, and a block of cheese and set them on the counter. "I'm cooking. Omelets sound okay?"

"You don't have to cook for me." Emma grabbed a skillet from a cabinet and set it on the stove. "That's all me. They've been gone for a couple of months already."

"You've been in Staunton for two months?"

"About that." She shrugged. "My parents are on the trip of a lifetime. I don't know when they'll return."

An uncomfortable silence lingered between them for the briefest of moments, until Adam hip-bumped her lightly to step into her place in front of the stove. He turned on a burner and dropped a pat of butter in the frying pan.

"Seriously, Adam, you don't have to cook for me. You're already going above and beyond."

He looked over at her and smiled his irresistible smile. "It's not a problem. I only ever get to cook for myself and I make way too much. This time I won't be forced to eat it all so it doesn't waste."

Emma chuckled. "You could make smaller amounts."

"You know I have five brothers, right?"

She shrugged. "Yeah. Of course, I do."

"By the time I actually got to eat anything I made, all five of them would have already sampled the food or downright stolen it from my plate. The only way to make sure I actually got enough was to cook a ton. Survival of the fittest and all that."

This time Emma laughed. "Growing up as an only child, I never had to worry about my food being stolen."

"Lucky," Adam said, dropping the sausages into the skillet. "So lucky."

"I always thought you were the lucky one." Emma leaned against the counter next to the sink. "I begged my parents for a brother or sister for years. I didn't understand until I became a teenager why they'd only ever had me."

Adam gave her a curious look. "They didn't just want one child?"

"No. Mom had always wanted a houseful of kids. Dad too. Unfortunately, Mom's health couldn't support that many pregnancies. She has an autoimmune disorder that showed itself while she was pregnant with me. I'm some kind of miracle baby. Everyone expected Mom to lose me before I could be born."

"So, you really have been stubborn your entire life," Adam said, giving her a wink.

Emma grabbed the dish towel and snapped it at him lightly. "I am not stubborn. I'm independent and strong willed."

Adam laughed. "Tell yourself whatever you need to in order to sleep at night."

Emma planted her hands on her hips. "If I'm stubborn, you're infuriating."

"Hey, I resemble that remark." Adam scooped the sausages out of the pan and put them on a plate. Grabbing a knife from the butcher block, he quickly chopped them up into small sections, then diced an onion and dropped the pieces into the skillet with a new pat of butter.

"My sources confirm this to be true."

"You have spies watching me?" Adam asked as he moved the onion around in the pan.

"They aren't spies! More like—sources."

"You say tomato and I'll say potato."

"Um, that's not exactly how that goes," Emma said.

Adam shrugged and grinned. "Says who?"

"Ugh." Emma rolled her eyes for about the hundredth time since she'd shown up in his office. Just like when they were kids. "See? You are infuriating."

"I'm adorable, actually. My mom says so all the time." He looked around the kitchen. "Do you have a cheese grater?"

"It's in the cabinet up there to your left." She pointed to the correct cabinet. Adam opened it up and found the tool he needed.

"Do you like your eggs really cheesy?" he asked as he shredded the brick of cheddar cheese.

"Who doesn't?" Emma opened the refrigerator and pulled out a jar of salsa and a container of sour cream. "How about we go western with the omelets?"

Adam nodded approval as he stirred the onions. "Sounds

good to me."

Emma set the two toppings on the counter. "So, do you think we scared the hit man off?"

Adam looked at her, his expression serious. "Truthfully?"

She nodded despite knowing she probably didn't really want to hear his answer.

"No. He might take a break tonight, but you are on his radar and not killing you now would make him look bad to the business."

"So, not killing me makes him look bad. Killing me will make him a hero?" Emma frowned.

Adam cracked some eggs into the pan, tossing the shells into the sink. "You know how cartels and gangs work. It will elevate his status. Earn him approval from the bosses."

She sighed. "Yay, me."

Adam reached over and covered her hand with his. Out of habit, Emma turned her hand palm up so their fingers intertwined. They'd held hands so many times as children before it became taboo in middle school. She'd missed the simple touch. He squeezed lightly. "I'm not going to let anything happen to you."

Emma looked down at their joined hands. "I'm not sure if I'm supposed to feel this way or not, but I've really missed you."

"I've really missed you too, Emma." The intensity of his stare as he looked into her eyes sent a warm flush to her cheeks.

The food in the frying pan started popping and snapping, ending the moment.

Emma laughed, pulling her hand from his hold. "You going to finish that omelet before I starve to death?"

Adam chuckled as he picked up a spatula. "We don't want that happening after you already defied death twice today. One omelet à la Marshall coming right up."

* * *

He caught the hint of a blush that colored Emma's cheeks as he turned her omelet over. His hand still held a slight tingle where it had made contact with hers. So many years had passed and yet it seemed like barely a moment in time had separated them. No one had affected him the way Emma always had.

Sprinkling some cheese on top of the omelet, he scooped it up with a spatula and put it on a plate. "Dinner is served, m'lady." Adam set the plate on the small kitchen table with a deep bow.

"Why, thank you, kind sir," Emma responded with a curtsey and waited as Adam pulled her seat out from the table for her. She spooned some salsa, then some sour cream onto the steaming food. "That smells absolutely divine."

"Just give me two minutes to whip up another one and I'll join you." He stepped back to the stove and cracked four eggs into the pan, scrambling them up with a fork. When the eggs started to show signs of cooking through, he added sausage, onions, and cheese before flipping half the eggs over the top of it all. Piling some cheddar jack cheese on top, he waited a moment for it to melt before putting his food on a plate and joining Emma at the table.

Just as he sat, she rose. "I'm going to get us some orange juice."

Adam nodded as he shoveled a forkful of the eggs into his mouth, promptly spitting them out on his plate. "Holy moly, those are hot!"

Emma laughed as she poured two glasses of juice. "You are the one that just took them out of the pan."

"I know." Adam waved a hand in front of his mouth to cool it. "I'm just so darn hungry that I guess I forgot."

She placed a glass on the table in front of him. "Here. This will help the burn. Use the sour cream to cool the eggs down."

Adam took a long swallow of the icy-cold orange juice, then spooned two large dollops of salsa on his eggs followed by a scoop of sour cream.

"How long will your parents be gone?" he asked around a much cooler bite of food.

"Six months. Maybe longer," Emma replied. "Like I said, it's their trip of a lifetime."

"That's quite an excursion."

"Mom waited thirty-five years for Dad to retire, and they plan to make the most of it. That's what she told me when she asked me to drop my entire life and move back home." Emma took another bite of her eggs. "These really are delicious. Thanks for cooking."

"Remember the story of my five brothers and survival of the fittest?"

Emma nodded.

"Learning to cook was necessity rather than preference.

If you missed dinner, that's it. Leftovers never happened in our house."

"So, you cooked or starved?"

"Exactly." Adam shoved another forkful of eggs in his mouth.

Emma took a drink of juice. "Mom had dinner on the table every night at six. Dad got home at five thirty. You could have set a clock by our routine. It's one of the things I couldn't wait to escape. Routine is so mundane."

"So you ran off to the big city to live the life of an investigative reporter." It wasn't a question. Everyone in Staunton knew she'd left without looking back.

Emma shrugged. "I had to get away. Go somewhere that everyone didn't know my family."

"Richmond isn't that far away," Adam said.

"No. But it gave me enough distance to be who I am, not who everyone thought I should be."

And got her far away from him and all the memories. Miranda's death. Their failed relationship. Any chance of him ever winning over her heart....

"Now you're back in town and on a major cartel hit list. Exciting enough for you here yet?"

He meant it as a joke but the words just sort of fell flat on the table between them.

She stood up and carried her plate to the sink, where she rinsed it and put it in the dishwasher. "I was never looking for excitement, Adam. I just needed space to breathe. And no, I had no intention of witnessing a murder today. I just wanted to write a story about a drug drop."

"I'm sorry, Emma. I didn't mean it how it sounded." Adam shoved the last bit of his eggs into his mouth.

She shook her head, leaning against the counter and crossing her arms over her chest. "I'm sorry too. My nerves are totally shot. It's making me extra touchy, I guess."

Adam walked over to the sink and rinsed his plate, setting it in the dishwasher with Emma's. "It's been a long day. I think we're both a little on edge."

The dogs started barking. Emma walked toward the back door. "I better let the dogs in."

A loud bang sounded against the back door, followed by crazy dog barking. Emma's face turned pale. "Did you hear that?"

Adam held a finger to his lips and nodded.

The dogs barked, louder and crazier.

Emma made a move to go to the door, but Adam put a hand on her arm. "Wait here," he whispered, reaching for the gun on his hip and grabbing a flashlight off a wall charger in the corner of the kitchen.

CHAPTER 6

Adam pulled his gun from the holster as he moved quietly down the hallway toward the family room where the back door was located. The barking didn't let up as he approached the door, gun drawn in front of him.

Another loud bang sounded, but this time it seemed further away. The dogs quieted down some.

"That one was the back gate," Emma whispered behind him. "Sometimes the wind catches it, and that's the sound it makes."

Adam nodded. "Didn't I tell you to wait in the other room?"

"You actually meant it?" She looked surprised.

"Well, yeah."

Emma chuckled quietly. "That's so cute."

"At least stay behind me." He should have known she'd never listen to him. Adam turned so that his body mostly blocked hers as they moved slowly through the family room.

Emma did as he asked and followed close on his heels as they made it to the door. Adam used the barrel of his weapon to move the blinds enough that he could see out into the yard.

"Do you see anything?" Emma whispered behind him, her breath warm on his neck.

"No," he replied.

One of the dogs let out a little yip that made them both jump. "That's just Ricky. He's a yipper."

Adam nodded, his hand on the doorknob. "Stay down and out of sight, okay?"

"Fine." Emma moved over behind the sofa that faced the door and ducked down.

Stepping to the side of the door, he yanked it open and held his breath, waiting for gunfire. The only thing that came through that door were two balls of fur, scampering and barking as they passed through the room.

"Ricky! Lucy!" Emma scooped the two pups up in her arms and hugged them close. They covered her face with licks as she giggled. "You scared us so much."

"Keep the dogs in here with you," Adam said. "I'm going to close the door when I go outside to look around."

"Okay. Be careful. Please."

Gun out in front of him, Adam leaned over and peered into the backyard. Everything appeared quiet. Stepping through the door, he shone the flashlight all around. The large fenced-in area looked empty. Moving cautiously, he checked the side of the house and then the gate. The latch hung from the gate by one screw, and the door moved slightly in the breeze. Adam shone his light on the ground around the entryway, stopping when he caught sight of a perfectly formed shoeprint in the soft dirt.

By the size and the smooth, slightly pointed impression, it appeared to be a man's dress shoe, but he'd need to get the crime scene tech out to the yard to examine it to know for sure.

Pulling out his cell phone, he first snapped a few pictures of it, then sent them with a text to the tech on call, asking her to come and check it out. She responded immediately, letting him know she was on her way. He sent the same photo and a text to his lieutenant to keep him in the loop.

Adam headed back into the house. When he made it to the patio at the door, he caught sight of a paper bag full of something on the cement. Using the flashlight, he looked into the open top of the bag and spotted a rock and a piece of paper.

"Hey, Emma? Do you have any gloves in the first aid kit?"

Emma stuck her head out the door. "You need gloves? For what?"

"Our visitor may have left us a gift." He pointed at the brown bag. "I want to check it out but not touch it in case there are fingerprints."

"Okay. Be right back."

Adam continued to survey the area, finding a mark in the trim around the door where the rock probably had hit. That would have definitely set the dogs barking. Thankfully, they were so distracted by the bag, they didn't notice the open back gate. He'd have to remember to tell Emma the latch was broken before she let them out again.

Emma reappeared in the doorway and handed Adam some blue gloves. "What do you think is in the bag?"

Adam handed the flashlight to Emma and pulled on the gloves, one at a time. The porch light provided enough illumination for him to see the bag's contents. "Let's find out."

He leaned over and pulled the top of the bag as open as he could and reached in, pulling out the rock that sat at the bottom. A white piece of paper had been wrapped around it and held in place with a rubber band. Removing the rubber band, he peeled the paper away and turned it over. A small photograph of Adam and Emma sitting in the kitchen eating their omelets fell from the folded paper.

Emma leaned over to pick it up, but Adam stopped her. "Don't. Let me. It could have prints on it, remember?"

"Oh, right. Sorry." She stood back up.

Adam picked up the photo instead, resting it on the rock in his hand. "How did he manage this?"

"I know how," Emma said. "There's a new gadget that you can use to print digital pictures from your cell phone. It's kind of like a Polaroid camera—instant gratification. What I don't understand is why he'd watch us eat, take a picture, then throw it at us. Why not just shoot me through the window?"

"He's sending a message. Letting us know he's in charge. That he can get to you anytime he wants and is enjoying the little game of cat and mouse that has developed."

"He's taunting me?"

Adam nodded. "I'm afraid so."

Emma rubbed her hands over her face. "What do we do now?"

Adam returned the rock and the note to the paper bag. "We need to figure out a safe place for you to go."

"I can't leave the dogs."

"I know," Adam replied. "Once crime scene gets here, I'll come inside, and we can figure it out together. I have to stay out here until Vonda arrives."

Emma rubbed her hands up and down her arms. "It sure did get cold. I'll go start a pot of coffee."

"Perfect. Thanks. Just stay away from uncovered windows, okay?"

As Emma disappeared back into the house, Adam pulled his phone from his pocket and dialed the station.

"Staunton police. Non-emergency line. How can I help you?"

"Hey, Simmons. It's Marshall. I'm going to give you an address. Can you send a car over to sit on the place tonight? Someone is stalking the resident and I'm pretty sure the person will try to come back here."

"Sure thing, Detective. As soon as you give me the address, I'll send a car on over."

"Thanks." He gave Simmons the address and disconnected the call.

This thing with Emma had gotten too serious too quickly. Whoever it was she'd seen killed, they must have been mixed up with some really bad people.

A flash of light, accompanied by the sound of an engine, caught Adam's attention. A car door slammed. He drew his gun and moved to the side of the house where he could see over the fence.

"Hello?" a voice called. "Detective Marshall?"

"Back here, Vonda! Follow the fence around until you find a gate. The latch is busted. You might want to check it for fingerprints. There's a footprint that I marked over there too."

"Always the thorough one," Vonda replied, stepping through the gate, flashlight in one hand and toolbox in the other. "There's a good-sized scuff mark just below the handle on the outside. I'm guessing your perp kicked this sucker open."

Adam frowned as he studied the mark. "Those dogs were so loud, we never heard it."

Vonda shrugged. "They probably heard him coming and tried to tell you. What else you got?"

"Over by the back door." He pointed to the house. "There's a brown paper bag with a rock and a photograph inside."

"So, the perp kicked open the gate *Pulp Fiction*-style, then tossed you a note and took off?" Vonda walked across the yard, using her flashlight to check the ground as she walked.

"That's what I'm thinking. And before you ask, I've got Emma in protective custody for the night. We are not on a date or anything."

Vonda looked at him over her shoulder. "Why would I even care?"

"The photo inside the bag shows us eating dinner in

her kitchen."

She set her tool kit down on the patio and turned to face him. "I'm just here for the evidence, Detective. What you do in your off time ain't none of my business. What I am wondering is why some dude came blasting through here like he's in the next *Die Hard* movie to leave you a picture of yourself."

"You're a bit of an action movie buff, aren't you?"

"I'm not asking you what you do on your off time, so don't ask me." Vonda pulled on a pair of gloves and took out her camera to take a couple pictures of the patio and the bag.

Adam raised his hands in mock surrender. "Sorry. Didn't mean to offend."

"You're good." She picked up the bag and examined it. Grabbing her camera, she snapped a few pictures of the outside, then pulled out the contents, setting all three items on the patio table. "Nice pic of you, Detective. Perp got your good side."

Adam peered over her shoulder. "All you can see is my shoulder and the side of my head."

Vonda chuckled. "I know."

The door opened, and Emma stepped out carrying two mugs of hot coffee. "Oh! I didn't realize we had a visitor."

"Emma Thomas, this is Vonda Luray, one of our crime scene technicians."

Vonda gave Emma a quick glance. "Nice to meet you, miss."

Emma handed one of the cups to Adam, then offered the other to Vonda. "Nice to meet you as well. Coffee?"

She pointed to the door. "I've got cream and sugar inside."

"I'm good, honey. Thanks so much." Vonda went back to her work.

"What should I do?" Emma asked Adam. "Do you need me out here or can I go inside?"

Emma had a little hint of something he couldn't quite decipher in her voice. Her glance kept moving to Vonda and then back to him like she wanted to keep an eye on the other woman. If he didn't know better, he'd think Emma might be a tiny bit jealous.

"You can go on inside. No reason for us both to be cold. I'll be in when Vonda's done processing the scene."

"Won't be too long," Vonda said from over by the gate where she dusted for fingerprints. "You'll have your man back all warm and cozy in no time."

"Oh, no," Emma said, her face turning a warm shade of crimson. "Adam's not my man. "

Adam laughed, enjoying her embarrassment a bit more than he probably should have. "You don't have to sound so disgusted by the idea."

Emma's flush deepened. "I didn't mean—"

Vonda gave Adam a big grin. "Detective Marshall here's a fine-lookin' man. Even if he is a little uptight for my own tastes."

"I'm not uptight! I'm just reserved."

Vonda made a little clicking noise with her tongue. "Reserved? Is that what they call it now when someone is strung tighter than that tiny string on a violin?"

"Don't you have some prints to finish lifting?" Adam asked

as Vonda laughed.

"You can't hurry art." She pulled a piece of tape off a large roll. "But don't worry, I'll be out of your hair in a minute or two."

"I'm just going to feed the dogs and clean up in the kitchen. Thanks for coming out here to do this." Emma pulled open the door and disappeared inside the house.

"She's cute. No wonder you like her," Vonda said casually as she brushed some more powder on the gate.

"It's not like that. We know each other from high school."

"I hope you know her well. 'Cause from where I'm sittin', it looks like that woman's got some secrets."

Adam shrugged. They all did. "I don't know about secrets, but she does have the local drug cartel after her."

"And so you've gone all *Romancing the Stone* and plan to protect her."

"I see you're still speaking in movie titles."

Vonda laughed and motioned around the yard. "This job is just a stepping stone in my career. I want to consult on action movies one day."

"And leave all that Staunton has to offer behind?"

She shrugged. "I just want something more."

Almost the same thing Emma had said about leaving Staunton. He loved his hometown and didn't understand a need to escape it but apparently it really was a thing.

"Hello?" a voice called from the dark. "Detective Marshall?"

"Follow the fence but don't touch the gate when you pass through. It's covered in black powder," Vonda answered for him.

A few seconds later, a young officer entered the yard. "Hey, Vonda," he said when he saw her, passing a look of admiration in her direction.

Vonda gave him a slight nod as she pressed a piece of lifting tape to the gate handle. "Sawyer."

The officer walked over to where Adam stood on the patio. He looked confused. "You needed backup, sir?"

"I'm on a protective detail. Can you hang out here until Vonda's done working the scene?"

"Sure thing, sir."

"Don't call me sir. I work for a living."

Sawyer's very fair face flushed a bright red. "Sorry, s—I mean, Detective."

Adam clapped him lightly on the shoulder, then pulled open the back door. "Thanks, kid."

* * *

Emma stood in the kitchen when the police car pulled up. As she decided to go and see why, she heard the back door open.

"Emma?"

"In here!"

Adam filled the doorway with his broad, muscular shoulders, the room overflowing with his strength and presence. She sucked in a breath as her heart rate kicked up a notch. For a quick moment, she forgot that the only reason Adam stood there was because someone wanted to kill her. They weren't young and innocent anymore. The relationship they'd had was over and done with years ago.

His intensity as he looked at her set all the butterflies that had recently moved in to her abdomen in flight. She quickly quieted them down with a reminder of why she and Adam could never go down that road.

"Di—did something else happen?" Emma finally remembered how to make words again.

"No?" Adam sounded confused. "Why?"

Emma motioned out the window. "The police just showed up."

Adam smiled, the warmth of it washing over her and making her think things she shouldn't—like how nice it would be to lean into his chest and feel the strength of his arms wrapped around her.

"Officer Sawyer is going to hang out with the crime scene tech so I can be inside with you. I don't want you out of my sight any longer than necessary until we find this guy."

"I hope it won't take too long." Emma regretted the words immediately. She made it sound like she didn't want Adam around, which had become the furthest thing from the truth. Even if she had no right to feel that way

Adam smiled, maybe with a tiny hint of sadness. She couldn't be sure; it had been so fleeting. "We'll get your life back as quickly as we can. I know I'm the last person you want hanging around all the time."

Stepping closer, Emma put a hand on Adam's arm. "I don't feel that way at all."

There went that hint of sadness in his smile again.

"You don't have to do that. I understand. It's scary having someone want you dead."

The back door opened. "Hey, Detective! You got a sec?" a male voice called.

"That's Sawyer, the patrol officer I requested. I'll be right back."

Emma took a long, deep breath in an attempt to steady herself. She'd not been entirely honest with Adam. Having him around all the time wasn't easy. There were so many things he didn't know about adult Emma. Things that didn't fit with the young, stars in her eyes version of Emma that Adam had always known. Things that would change the way Adam saw her forever.

It was selfish, she knew it, especially when her heart skipped a beat or two whenever he touched her, no matter how casual the contact.

She'd gone to Adam for help. Yes, she'd witnessed a murder and Adam was a cop. But Staunton had many cops. She could have called 911. Running to Adam was purposeful—the perfect excuse to see him again after so many years.

Adam had been her first friend when her family had moved to Staunton. A shy second grader, Emma had had no idea how to make friends. When she fell on the playground and Adam was there, offering his hand to help her up, she knew in that moment that she'd always be able to count on him.

If only Miranda hadn't decided that Adam would be her New Year's kiss. If only Emma had stopped Adam from kissing her under the mistletoe. Miranda wouldn't have seen it and taken off in her daddy's too-fast car. She wouldn't have lost control of that car and wrapped it around a tree. Emma's best girlfriend would still be alive, and Emma would have had no idea what it felt like to kiss the first man that had ever entered her heart.

Running off to school in Richmond after graduation let her escape the choices she'd made as a teen. Staying in Richmond to work for the local paper had only led to a series of even worse choices, things that had sent her back home with her tail between her legs under the guise of house sitting for her parents.

Mama had always said, what's done is done. Nothing would change the past, so Emma had to focus on the future. If she had one anymore—this story was supposed to be her big break back into freelancing.

She finished clearing up the dishes from dinner, pushing aside all thoughts of the past—even the recent past. As she dried her hands and turned off the light, Adam returned.

"Going to bed already?" he asked.

"Already?" Emma pointed to the clock on the microwave. "It's nearly midnight."

Moonlight poured in through the window over the sink, casting shadows over Adam's features. She couldn't tell if his eyes were dark from the shadows or from how close they stood. His breaths fanned lightly across her face, each one stepping her heart rate up just a little more.

He lifted his hand slightly, like he wanted to touch her, then dropped it back down to his side, his expression turning neutral. "I didn't realize how late it had gotten. The tech is finished up out back. Sawyer is stationed out front. I'll stay in the living room to keep an eye on the back door."

"Do you really think he will come back?" Emma asked.

Adam frowned. "I didn't think he'd come here tonight at all, so we can't assume anything. This guy means business."

Emma sighed and leaned on the counter, suddenly exhausted. "I can't believe I picked that moment to look in the window of the cabin. If I'd been ten minutes later—"

This time Adam did reach up and touch her cheek briefly. "You can't think like that. Everything happens for a reason."

"Did you just hear yourself?" Emma laughed. "You sound like my mother."

He shrugged. "It's true."

"I didn't take you for the God-has-a-plan type."

"I wouldn't exactly say that's my thought process. But I do believe in karma, and she has a serious beef with this guy."

"Yeah, I guess she does." Emma opened the refrigerator and grabbed a bottle of water. "I'll get you some blankets and a pillow for the couch."

"I don't need much. Not planning on sleeping anyway."

Emma stopped walking toward the hall and turned around to look at Adam. "You can't stay up all night."

"I'm not much of a sleeper. I'll be fine."

She didn't know if she should believe him or not. "I'll bring you a blanket and pillow anyway, just in case you change your mind."

Adam nodded. "Okay."

Emma heard Adam walk to the back of the house as she pulled open the door to the linen closet. She should have known when they were kids he'd grow up to be a police officer. Seeing him now as a grown man whose protective streak had morphed into a career of protecting and serving his town did fluttery things to her heart. Grabbing a soft quilt her grandmother had made many years ago, she went to her bedroom and got one of the extra pillows from her closet. All the years she'd been gone, and her parents hadn't changed a thing.

Carrying the items with her, Emma returned to the living room. Adam stood by the couch, a black bag open on the coffee table. He pulled his shirt up over his head, revealing trim, hard planes of muscle.

Emma sucked in a breath. Adam turned around, a look of surprise on his face as he held the shirt in front of him. "My other shirt had black fingerprint powder on the sleeve. That stuff gets everywhere."

It shouldn't have been a big deal. She'd seen Adam shirtless plenty of times at his parents' pool when they were teenagers. Adult Adam looked a lot different than teen Adam though.

A jagged scar ran from his navel up and over the rise of his right hip. Emma stepped closer, reaching out but not quite touching the raised skin. "What happened?"

Adam shrugged, quickly pulling another shirt over his head. "A guy brought a knife to a gunfight, and I wasn't fast enough with my gun."

"You were working when it happened?"

He nodded. "Yeah. About three years ago. Staunton had a run-in with a serial killer. The Blue Ridge Killer."

Emma lifted a hand to her mouth. "That was you? I mean, I read about the case but no one ever mentioned your name."

"There was an FBI Agent, Bill Ryan. It had been his case up until—Leslie. He deserved the glory for the capture. I wasn't interested in any of it."

"But with you in a relationship with Leslie, that's a huge detail of the case. It should have been all over the media."

"I asked them not to put my name in the police reports. And for once, people listened. Agent Ryan wanted the publicity. I didn't. It was—" Adam paused and took a deep breath. "I thought it might be easier on her family if my name wasn't connected to hers online for the rest of time, since her death had basically been my fault."

"Your fault? How—"

Adam held up a hand to stop her. "He took Leslie because he wanted to taunt me. I'd figured out who he was, and we were so close to stopping him. He killed her, then himself, leaving a full video confession to eight other murders as well as a recording of what he did to her."

"Did you love her?" Emma asked.

He shrugged. "We talked about getting married, having a family one day."

"But were you in love with her?"

Adam nodded. "I was. You were gone. I knew we'd never be together so I tried to move on."

"Oh, Adam."

He turned away, making a big deal out of folding his dirty shirt and setting it on the coffee table. "It's just the cost of doing business. Sometimes people in my line of work get hurt."

"That was so much more than sometimes people get hurt. How have you kept going? I think that would have ended me."

Adam turned back to face her. "I don't have a choice. What else would I do? Police work is what I know. I live with the knowledge every single day that I couldn't save her, but I had to go on."

Emma hugged the linens she held to her chest in an effort to resist wrapping her arms around Adam. The intensity of his stare could have rivaled any hurricane. "I'm so sorry you had to experience that."

Adam reached up and ran his fingertips lightly along the line of her jaw. He didn't want to talk about the killer or Leslie's death anymore. He had to focus on the current threat and preventing history from repeating itself. "It's life, Emma. Sometimes we get hit with a curve ball and it knocks us to the ground."

The tiny trail of sparks his touch left in its wake shot straight through her. As she handed the blanket and pillow to him, her hands shook. Instead of taking the bedding, he clasped her hands with his. "Your fingers are freezing."

"They always are. Except in July. Maybe August."

He set the pillow and blanket on the couch and rubbed her hands gently. "I don't remember you being like that when we were kids."

Emma shrugged one shoulder. "Things change. People change."

Adam looked at her curiously but let the subject, and her hands, go. "Thanks for the stuff. I think I'll watch a little television. Can you show me where your dad keeps the remote control?"

Emma reached into a drawer in the coffee table and pulled out two. She handed him a good-sized black one. "This controls everything. Except for the volume. You need this one." She handed him a smaller grey one. "I have no idea why, but we can't get that other one to change the sound."

"Got it." Adam grinned, his playful demeanor back in full force. "You need me to tuck you in now?"

Emma rolled her eyes, remembering how she couldn't fall asleep as a child unless her dad tucked the blankets in all around her. "I'm not twelve anymore, Adam. I can put myself to bed now."

He winked. "Just making sure. Since your mama and daddy are away and all."

She batted him with a throw pillow. "You're ridiculous."

"But also adorable."

She couldn't help but smile. He was way more than adorable. Adam had grown to be a full-blown hottie. "Good night, Adam."

"Good night, Emma! Sleep tight and don't let the bed bugs bite!" Adam called after her, repeating her father's nightly mantra. She cursed the day she'd ever told him about that bedtime ritual.

CHAPTER 7

Emma closed her bedroom door and leaned against it, willing her pulse to slow down. There hadn't been a man in her life since that night Adam kissed her. Oh, she'd dated, but no one had really won her over. They'd never stacked up to her first love. And as far as she could tell from what she'd seen and experienced since showing up at the police station that afternoon, there never would be anyone who could.

Adam had gotten finer with age in every way possible. His skinny boy frame had grown into perfection. The deepness of his voice was in high contrast to his middle school years, and the way her blood had burned when he touched her… well, that had definitely changed too.

"You're a hot mess, girl," she said to her reflection in the mirror over her dresser as she pulled out a pair of pajamas.

And, she was. In so many ways. Her hair was a matted knot. She'd probably just have to burn her clothes after all they'd been through that day. She couldn't imagine any of her mother's fancy smelling detergents getting the dirt, grass, and grease stains out of her shirt or her jeans, even if the denim hadn't torn across her knee.

The hot water of the shower felt amazing. Emma shampooed and then conditioned her hair, finger combing the tangled curls as she did. Muscles that had been tight, relaxed some. Her fall on the mountain had left her knees bruised, her face cut and her palms scraped up. The body wash burned slightly where her skin was raw. As she washed away the dirt of the day, her mind wandered back to the man sitting on her parents' sofa. How many times had they sat there together, watching a movie or yelling at a football game? She hadn't realized until that moment how much she'd missed her childhood best friend.

Except her body hadn't reacted to Adam like he was an old friend, the traitor.

She stayed in the shower so long, the water began to run cool. Shutting off the taps, Emma grabbed her towel and dried off before wrapping her hair in the towel and pulling on her pajamas.

Her joints ached, probably from all the running for her life she'd done that day. Not to mention the multiple tumbles she'd taken. All she wanted to do was collapse in bed and pass out, but her mind had switched to hypervigilant mode. Not because her life was in danger but because the man she'd worked so hard to scrub from her heart and her mind had undone all her efforts with one easy smile and a couple innocent touches. If only she were the same woman she'd been when she left Staunton all those years ago, maybe she'd be enough for a man like Adam.

Pushing aside all thoughts of the way his scent had

wrapped itself around her in the kitchen, making it hard to keep her words coherent, Emma crawled into her bed and pulled the covers up to her chin.

Tomorrow she had to find a place for the dogs to stay for a couple of days. Then she had to figure out where to go herself. It wasn't fair to expect Adam to guard her day and night.

As her eyes slowly closed and she drifted off to sleep, her thoughts traveled back to that night so long ago. She could almost feel his arms wrapped around her, the safe feeling she'd always had with her oldest friend taunting her. Maybe it wouldn't be so bad if Adam did have to watch over her day and night. Just for a little while.

* * *

Adam spent a good portion of the night after Emma went to bed reliving the night of Leslie's murder. All the anger and sadness he'd worked so hard to lock away made an appearance as the events of that night marched through his brain like a movie reel. Leslie's lifeless body, the killer dead beside her and the video confession. How many times had he tortured himself watching that video looking for some way he could have saved Leslie?

Agent Ryan had been beyond angry at Adam for getting to the crime scene first. He'd been working the Blue Ridge Killer case for months, so Adam understood his thirst for blood and glory, sort of. At least no more women would die and he could go home and nurse his broken heart and mourn the loss of the woman he loved.

Sometime around sunrise, his demons finally settled back into the chest he reserved for them in the back of his mind. Stretching as he rose to his feet, Adam did a quick once over of the doors and windows then headed to the bathroom.

A light bang sounded at the back of the house. Adam stopped and listened. It sounded again. Grabbing his gun and slipping his feet into his boots, Adam walked quietly to the back door and looked between two slats on the blinds. The sun had barely begun to peek up over the horizon, so it was hard to see the entire backyard, even with the outside lights turned on.

There it went again. Soft, steady, and distant. He moved to the front of the house and looked out the kitchen window, just in case he'd misheard the noise.

It sounded the same there as it had in the living room. Working hard to be extra quiet, he punched in the alarm code, unlocked the front door and slipped outside. A neighborhood cat ran out of the driveway and into the street. A stiff breeze kicked up, but it didn't seem to stop the birds that had begun their morning chorus. The sun had finally made it up over the horizon, glazing the dew-covered yard in shades of pink.

Checking behind the bushes in front of the house first, Adam moved steadily around the perimeter of the house, checking anywhere someone could hide. When he'd circled all the way around the fenced-in backyard and came up on the side of the house by the garage, he found the garbage can with its lid hanging open, tapping against the side of the can every time the breeze passed through.

He tucked his gun into the holster on his belt and lifted the lid to close it. When he was done, he followed the garage wall to the front of the house, checking the ground for unusual prints as he walked. Rounding the corner of the garage, eyes still searching the ground, he ran straight into someone running at him. The impact knocked him to the ground.

His head whacked hard against the driveway, and his world went black. When Adam next opened his eyes, Emma stared down at him, a sleepy smile on her lips and worry in her eyes. Her curls tumbled around her shoulders in wild disarray, and she had a pink line on the side of her face from where it had lain on the pillow. He reached up and toyed with one of the curls.

"So beautiful. I always wondered if your hair felt like silk. It doesn't. It's softer."

"Are you okay?" Emma's face turned a sweet shade of pink as she smiled down at him. She pressed a palm to his face. "I'm so sorry."

"My head hurts," Adam said, reaching to probe his tender scalp with his fingers. "What happened? Did the guy whack me on the head?"

Emma sat back on her heels and gave him a funny look. "What guy? Was someone here again last night?"

Adam pushed himself up into a sitting position, resting his back against the garage door. "I don't know. I heard a noise, so I came out here to investigate. Next thing I knew I'd walked into someone and then blacked out."

"You walked into me. When I woke up and you were gone, but your truck was still here and the front door was unlocked, I panicked. Ran outside searching for you. When I ran around the corner, you were looking at something and didn't even see me."

"I was looking for shoeprints."

Emma smiled. "I'm sorry I knocked you over." She reached behind him and ran her fingers lightly over the back of his head, pausing when they made contact with the sore spot. "Let's go inside and put something cold on that lump."

The second her fingers made contact with his head, his pulse rate kicked up several notches. Now he couldn't tell if the dizziness he felt came from the head wound or the reaction to her touch. Adam wrapped his hand lightly around Emma's wrist. Her skin felt nearly as soft as her hair. "I just need a second to look at something. You go on inside and I'll meet you there."

She looked worried. "Are you sure you don't need me to help you inside? That was a nasty spill."

Adam chuckled. "Wasn't the first time I've banged my head, and I am one hundred percent certain it won't be the last." He squeezed her hand lightly. "I'll be fine. I promise. I just have to make sure that the back gate is secure before we leave today. Sawyer won't be back until tonight and only if I ask for him."

Emma nodded, but he could see the reluctance to leave him in her expression. He just needed five minutes to pull himself together, as much as from her proximity as his whack to the head.

"Fine. But if you aren't back in five minutes, I'm coming out after you." Emma crossed her arms over her chest, assuming the same stance her mother always had when they were kids to show she meant business.

Adam gave her a mock salute. "Yes, ma'am, Ms. Thomas."

She rolled her eyes at him for about the tenth time in the last twenty-four hours, then looked at an imaginary watch on her wrist. Some things apparently never changed. She tapped her wrist with one finger. "I mean it. Five minutes."

"Will do." Using the garage door handle to help, Adam pulled himself to his feet. The ground felt unsteady as he stood there, trying to calm the nausea that had kicked into high gear once he'd moved.

Emma tilted her head slightly and stared straight into his eyes. "Your pupils look fine, but I don't know, you're a little green around the gills. You sure you're okay?"

"I'm sure. Now go on inside. I don't like you out here so exposed like this. Lock the door again."

"What about you?"

"I'll go to the back door after I secure the gate and knock twice, pause, then knock again."

He knew the second she remembered their secret knock and all those nights she'd slipped out her bedroom window to walk through the woods and talk about their dreams. Her green eyes sparkled, emphasizing the gold flecks buried in the green irises just like the first day they met. Those exotic eyes had always mesmerized him. "Okay."

Adam watched as Emma disappeared back into the house.

Moving cautiously to make sure his balance held out, Adam walked back to the fence gate and stepped inside the yard. Pushing the gate closed, he jammed some rocks into the ground in front of it, then found a couple of thin branches that had fallen from the crepe myrtle trees recently and jammed them into the handle and latch. Finally, he moved a heavy pot with a hibiscus bush in it over in front of the gate. If anyone else tried to come in that way, at least he'd hear them coming.

His head throbbed by the time he finished. "Do you have any headache meds?" he asked Emma when he went back inside.

"In the hallway bathroom." She pointed in the general direction. "Should be in the medicine cabinet."

"Thanks." After he grabbed a couple tablets and a glass of water, Adam sat down at the kitchen table.

"I'm really sorry I knocked you down like that," Emma said, setting a cup of coffee on the table in front of him and handing him a bag of frozen peas.

"What's this for?" he asked, nodding at the peas as he accepted them.

"That knot on your head."

"It's my own fault for not watching where I was going." Adam held the peas to his head as he took a sip of the hot, dark liquid. "Good brew. I've never been a fan of those fancy single-cup machines. Nothing beats coffee grounds in a drip pot."

Emma laughed. "I kind of like my fancy single-cup machine. I'd have used it today but it's packed in a box in

Mom and Dad's garage."

Adam raised his cup. "I stand corrected. After last night, we really need to get you somewhere safe while I figure out who you saw killed yesterday."

"I know. Last night, while you were outside, I looked in Mom's address book and found the name of the kennel she uses. We can bring the dogs in this morning. I explained that I had an unexpected work emergency and they were very understanding."

"Work emergency?" Adam nodded. "Yeah, I guess that fits. I'd like to take a quick hot shower and get a change of clothes before we leave, if that's okay?"

"Absolutely. I'll pack a bag while you do that." Emma pointed to his head. "Are you sure we don't need to get that checked out?"

He pretended to rap on his head with his knuckles. "Hard as a rock. I'm good."

She looked skeptical but she let it drop. "There's towels in the cabinet under the sink. Toiletries too, if you need them."

"I've got everything I need but the towel. Thanks." He finished his cup of coffee in one long swallow. "Meet you back here in twenty?"

"Sounds good." Emma took his empty cup and rinsed it before setting it in the dishwasher. "I didn't even think to ask—did you want some breakfast? I don't usually eat until a little later in the morning, so it slipped my mind."

"The coffee was good for now. We can grab something later when we both get hungry."

"Okay," Emma replied.

Adam headed to the living room to grab his go bag. He needed hot water on his aching body right away. Between the night on the couch and the impromptu nap in the driveway, everything felt tight and sore. Not a bit of that had anything to do with Emma, he told himself one more time. Maybe he'd start to believe it eventually.

His only focus should be on keeping Emma safe and finding out who wanted her dead before they tried to kill her again.

CHAPTER 8

The extra-hot shower worked out some of the kinks but Adam still felt a little sore as he pulled on his clean clothes. Not exactly prime for a hike up a mountain. Unfortunately, that was exactly what he had to do. It had been too dark the night before to really see anything in the cabin. Once he got Emma settled in a hotel, he'd head on up there.

His phone vibrated on the counter where he'd set it before getting in the shower. Recognizing the number as his lieutenant, Bill Waters, he answered the call. "Hey, boss."

"Heard you had quite a night, Marshall."

That was putting it mildly for sure. "Ah, you know. Nothing out of the ordinary."

"Oh, so you get shot at regularly while buying produce?" Waters asked, chuckling.

"Keeps the shopping interesting."

"And what about the other call? The one with the intruder?"

"They're actually related, sir. Remember the woman that came by the station yesterday to report witnessing a murder?

Someone really wants her dead now."

"She okay?" Waters asked. "How'd she get herself in this kinda hot water?"

"The woman—her name is Emma—is an investigative journalist and she's been writing a piece on Staunton and the Blue Ridge Parkway."

"The rumors about the drug transports? Isn't that your case with the task force?"

"Yeah. A source she won't divulge—"

"Of course she won't." Waters sounded skeptical.

"The source told her about a cabin on a mountain that is supposed to be a drop spot. She hiked up there and just happened to look in the window when some guy shot another one in the head."

Waters grunted. "She really had no idea what she was walking into?"

Adam tossed his toiletries into his go bag and zipped the bag. "I'm convinced she didn't."

"And that somehow turned into a gunfight at the grocery store?"

"The shooter heard Emma and chased her down the mountain, but she managed to get away. He shot out a window in her car but missed Emma. She came straight to the station from there. I was taking her home to her parents' house when we stopped to get a few things. A minute or so after we entered the building, the guy also showed up at the store. He must have been following us."

"Are you absolutely certain this Emma isn't on the take with the cartel?" Waters asked. "I'm sending a team up to the cabin today."

"Why would they be trying to kill her if she were working with them?" Adam replied. "Besides, I've known Emma and her family most of my life."

"Just because you went to preschool together doesn't mean she's one of the good guys," Waters said. "But if you're positive, then keep doing what you're doing. If they are coming after her, we might be able to get to them."

His boss could be so cynical. "Exactly what I've been thinking. Right now, I'm going to get her stashed somewhere safe and then head up to the mountain to do a little looking around. Can we hold off on a team until I get a better look around in the daylight?"

"Sounds good," Waters replied. "Just keep me in the loop."

"Will do, sir." Adam disconnected the call.

Adam ran his hand through his wet hair in an attempt to tame the waves. The action was completely futile. Wet strands curled around his ear and dropped into his collar. He really needed to make time for a haircut in the near future.

He found Emma still in the kitchen, sitting at the table with a coffee mug in her hands. The curtains over the sink had been drawn closed. Smart woman. She looked up when he entered the room and smiled.

"I heard you talking to yourself in the bathroom."

Adam chuckled. "That was me on the phone with the lieutenant. He heard about the shooting last night."

"Ah." Emma took a drink from the mug. "He thinks I'm lying about not knowing anything."

Adam frowned. "What makes you say that?"

She stood up and walked to the sink where she rinsed her mug. "I would think I was lying. I mean, a guy gets murdered at exactly the same time I happen upon the cabin?"

He walked over to where she stood, turned her around so she faced him, and lifted her chin to meet his gaze. "No one thinks you're lying. If anything, you've given us the break we need to infiltrate the group and take them down. I'd have never known about that cabin if not for you."

"I never expected for us to cross paths again. I stayed away for so long, mostly because I was avoiding you. And now look at where we're at. I'm not the same person I was when I left." Emma fiddled with one of the buttons on his shirt; her eyes were filled with a dozen different emotions, none of which he could identify. Suddenly very aware of how close she was, his heart skipped a little beat as his pulse sped up. His nerve endings stood at attention, ready to feel her lips pressed to his. All they needed was a little sprig of mistletoe and it could have been that night all over again.

"I'm sorry you felt you had to stay away." Adam stepped in a little bit closer. Emma looked up at him again. "But I'm glad you've come back."

She pressed her palms to his chest lightly, as though trying to keep some space between them. "It's only temporary. I'm just here until my parents are done travelling. There are so many reasons why I can't stay." Her eyes glistened with moisture and darkened with the secrets he knew she guarded closely. Something had happened to Emma in the time she'd been gone, something more than witnessing an execution.

"You're here now. Let's concentrate on figuring out what you've gotten involved in." The desire to kiss her gripped him tightly, but he held back. He couldn't totally read Emma, and the last thing he needed to do was mess things up again. She needed him to keep her safe, and that was it. For the moment, at least. He took a reluctant step back. Maybe once he knew no one wanted her dead, he could focus on repairing their friendship. "And we have a murderer to find."

The flash of relief that lit her green eyes briefly as he moved away from her stabbed at his heart. A reminder that he needed to keep things professional—their friendship as it had been no longer existed.

"I put my bags by the door." Emma pointed toward the front hall. "I'll get the dogs on their leashes and meet you out front."

Adam nodded. "I'll grab my bag and yours. Make sure you lock up every door and window."

Emma nodded and disappeared, grasping the dog leashes so tightly, her knuckles turned white.

Going back to the living room, Adam picked up his bag then grabbed Emma's. His head ached a little still but nothing he couldn't live with. He'd worked through worse playing high school football.

Now the ache in his chest—that was a completely different story.

***

Emma's heart still pounded as she gathered up the pups and attached their leashes. Adam had been about to kiss her, and she'd really wanted him to. Kissing Adam would be a huge mistake, because she didn't think she could stop with just one, and getting involved with anyone, even her childhood sweetheart, would be a bad idea. She needed to be strong.

Strong enough to survive this life-or-death debacle she'd gotten herself into. After what had happened in Richmond, she had a lot to figure out for herself before she could give anything to anyone else.

"Come on, dogs." Emma led the little pups around the house as she checked doors and windows. Everything seemed secure, so she grabbed her purse and headed outside.

Adam stood beside the passenger door, looking at his phone. As she and the dogs approached, he glanced up and smiled. "All set?"

Adult Adam had changed in so many ways from teenage Adam, but his smile had stayed exactly the same. Warm, genuine, a tiny bit teasing. It wrapped her in warmth and drew her in, no matter how much her brain said she should resist.

She smiled back. "As ready as I'll ever be."

He pulled open the back door of the crew cab, and Emma lifted the dogs inside. Adam opened her door and offered her a hand to get up inside. When she placed her hand in his, there was no denying the shock of electricity that shot through her. Adam felt it too. She could see it in his eyes. They stood there, locked in place. Emma tried to form words, say anything to move them forward, but her mouth wouldn't listen to her brain.

"Be careful of the running board." Adam broke the tension between them, pointing to the step up. He pressed a hand lightly to her lower back to guide her. "It gives a beast of a shin bruise if you miss it."

Emma nodded, quickly scrambling into the seat of the truck. Adam closed her door and she watched as he walked around to the driver side, willing her pounding heart to slow down in case Adam could hear it slamming against her chest.

"So, where're we headed?" Adam slid into the driver seat and closed the door.

Emma gave him the address.

"I know that place. It's not far from where I live." He put the truck in gear and backed out of the driveway.

Not far from where I live.

Emma had no idea where Adam lived. In fact, she realized she knew very little about him. Did he have a roommate? He'd had at least one serious relationship but other than that, she had no idea. Did he have any hobbies? A best friend? All the things she knew about Adam were in the past. Maybe he had changed completely. Maybe he lived like a slob, with dirty clothes and fast food wrappers strewn everywhere.

Emma looked over at the man beside her. The inside of his truck was pretty much spotless. So, his home probably would be too. His clothes looked neat and wrinkle free. The wavy hair she'd always loved was on the long side and still a little unruly the way it had been when they were teenagers but the rest of him had become more angular and chiseled. Light stubble lined a jaw she hadn't remembered being so strong and defined.

Adam glanced over at her. "You look pretty deep in thought. Want to talk about it?"

Before she could answer, the truck jolted forward, throwing her body against the tightening seat belt. Her head snapped back against the headrest. The dogs both let out a yelp. "What was that?"

"We've got company." Adam gripped the steering wheel harder. "Hold on."

He pressed the gas pedal to the floor, sending the truck flying forward. Emma watched the car behind them, a black SUV with tinted windows, in the side mirror. As Adam sped up, so did the SUV, slamming into them once more.

"This guy knows what he's doing. I'm going to have to try and lose him. I can't outrun him if I don't." Adam spun the wheel, turning right down a narrow road. The back of the truck fishtailed but quickly found traction as they sped along. The SUV made the turn at the last minute, rocking sideways on to two wheels momentarily. Adam kept his eyes forward. Emma watched as trees and houses sped by, praying they wouldn't encounter any innocent bystanders.

They made another quick turn to the left. Adam steered the car up an incline. "There's a dirt road up this way around a sharp bend that leads to an old fishing hole. No one knows it's there unless they know this area. I'm guessing our guy doesn't. If I can get enough distance between us, I can make the turn and get us lost in the trees."

"Just do what you have to. Don't worry about us." The dogs were cowering together on the floor in the back seat. Emma gripped the door handle and kept an eye on the side mirror. She caught sight of the SUV as it made the turn onto the narrow lane. Emma sucked in a breath. The driver almost lost control but regained it before he rolled.

Adam keyed his radio and gave their location, asking for backup. "There's a vehicle pursuing us. I'm going to try and lose them but in case I can't, send a car."

The dispatcher responded, "Ten-Four, Detective. I've got a unit headed up that way right now."

They sped up the mountain. Adam handled the curves and turns expertly, like he'd driven this road a hundred times. The SUV swerved and rocked behind them, the front right tire sliding off the edge of the road a few times and kicking up a cloud of dirt as the driver struggled to get back on the asphalt. As they rounded a sharp turn, Adam suddenly whipped the wheel to the left into a thick stand of trees.

"Hold on!" He floored the pedal and shot through a narrow opening in the tree line Emma never would have noticed if she was just driving by. Emma gripped the door handle as she bounced on the seat. Adam barely slowed as he plowed through the brush. When they reached a small clearing in front of a pond, he put the truck in park, turned it off, and jumped out. "Come on!"

"The dogs. I have to get the dogs!"

"They'll be fine. He's not trying to kill them!"

Emma jumped out of the truck, following Adam into the woods. He grabbed her hand and pulled her along with him.

"Stay close," he whispered.

"Where are we going?"

"Back to the main road to make sure he didn't follow us in here." Adam pushed a low-hanging branch out of the way and held it so it wouldn't hit her in the face. "This little trail runs along the road we just took. If he followed us, we'll see him before he sees us."

"What about your truck?" And her parents' dogs.

"He only wants you. If the truck is empty, he'll look for us. We'll have the upper hand this time."

They walked along in silence for the next few minutes, Adam forging the way through the overgrowth and Emma listening for the sound of a vehicle. All she heard were birds and insects going about their business. A siren sounded in the distance, growing louder as they drew closer to the main road.

Adam stopped walking and motioned through a little opening in the trees. There was the narrow roadway they'd been driving on. A police car, lights and sirens running, flew by them.

"He's gone?" Emma whispered.

Adam nodded. "I think so. The patrol unit will probably scare him off if he hasn't run already. I want to look around a little bit just to be sure there are no surprises. Can you stay here and watch the road?"

"Yes."

Adam started to move away from her, but Emma reached out and touched his arm. He stopped and looked at her, questions in his eyes.

"Be careful, okay? I couldn't handle it if—"

He ran his fingertips along the line of her jaw with a gentle smile. "I'm good, Emma. This is my job, remember?"

She nodded, and he disappeared into the woods. A couple small cars passed, heading up the hill while she waited. When ten minutes or so had passed, Emma noticed a black SUV slowly rolling by, heading down the mountain. She stepped back into the cover of the trees, afraid the driver would see her. But he didn't stop. He kept rolling slowly on down the road. She shifted to try and get a read on the license plate but only caught the first two letters, *SF*. A few seconds later, the police car returned and followed the direction the SUV had gone in.

Adam stepped up next to her, a finger over his lips. They both watched as the police car disappeared around the bend.

"Do you think he saw the path we took?" Emma asked.

Adam shook his head. "No. I went and made sure the tree branches had fallen back in place and covered the opening. If he'd noticed, he would be here looking for us."

Emma frowned and motioned to the road. "He just drove by before you got here, heading down the mountain."

"I don't think we need to worry, I'm sure he has seen the police car by now. He'll back off for a while."

"So, what do we do now?"

"We head back to the truck and hang out for a bit, just to be sure he's gone. Then we get those dogs to the kennel and you somewhere safe."

He took her hand and led the way back to the truck. This time though, he didn't let go. And neither did she. It made her feel safe. His strength and confidence seemed to radiate to her when they touched, and at the moment she could use a whole lot of strength and confidence.

CHAPTER 9

He felt the tremor when he grasped Emma's hand. She tried so hard to act tough but the whole someone-trying-to-kill-her thing was creating cracks in that defensive armor of hers. Whatever she had witnessed, it had to be major, because that guy wasn't giving up. And he was good at his job. Really good.

It didn't matter. Adam was good at his job too. Much better than some hired gun.

Even under the circumstances, holding Emma's hand felt right. Like they were meant to do that all the time. He'd given up on the idea of falling in love and having a family a long time ago. In the last twenty-four hours though, since Emma had shown up in his precinct, long-forgotten dreams had begun to surface again.

When they reached the little clearing, Emma let go of his hand and ran to the truck. He could hear the dogs yapping and yelping. Dogs were meant to bark. Not yap. If he ever got a dog, it would have some size and some power. Like a German shepherd or a Belgian Malinois. A man's dog, not a dog that wore little sweaters and rode around in a purse.

Emma opened the truck door and grabbed them both by the leash, letting them out of the vehicle. They led her around the clearing, sniffing and yapping as they stopped to do their business.

"Do you come out here often?" Emma motioned around the clearing.

"Often enough. When I need a little perspective."

"How did you even find it?" Emma leaned down to pet one of the dogs that had stretched out on her feet.

"It's my uncle's property."

She smiled and gave him a little wink. "Ah. The family hideaway. Is there some kind of hidden underground bunker here too?"

"Nah. Just an old hunting cabin on the other side of the pond."

"With bulletproof glass and escape hatches?" She teased him. Emma's smile lit up her green eyes, while the laughter added a natural blush to her porcelain skin.

"He is a bit of a prepper type. Belongs to this super-secret group of other apocalypse preppers."

"I knew it!" The morning sun hit the water of the pond at just the right angle to bring out the reddish gold highlights in her chestnut hair.

He now knew from past experience how soft and silky that hair was. His fingers itched to run through it. Adam shook his head to clear it. They'd shared one kiss. A stolen moment a dozen years ago. How could one instance of teenage desire define a man's entire life?

You sound like one of those silly romance novels Carrie reads.

His cousin Carrie had always been a hopeless romantic. She dreamed of handsome princes on strong white steeds sweeping in and rescuing her from little ole Staunton, Virginia. When she took the job as an airline flight attendant, Adam never expected her to end up with a real live prince.

"Whatcha thinking about, all serious like that?" Emma stood in front of him as the two dogs played chase around his ankles.

"Did you know Carrie married a prince?"

Emma's eyes widened in surprise. "Your cousin Carrie?"

"Yeah. Crazy, isn't it?"

She shrugged. "Not really. She always said she'd marry into royalty."

"He's from some bigwig oil family in the Middle East. I didn't want to like him, but I couldn't help it. He actually treats my cousin like a princess in every way."

Emma laid a hand on his shoulder. "Don't worry, Adam. Someday you will find your princess."

He laughed. "I'm too rough around the edges for crowns and balls and stuff."

The idea of falling in love didn't sound as bad as it used to though. Emma's sporadic touches had woken up a part of his brain that had long since gone dormant. As all of his high school and college buddies got married, Adam had always assumed he'd be the one to stay single—married to his job, Carrie had often said.

Especially after Leslie had been killed.

Maybe fate had decided to give him a second chance at happiness. He looked over at the woman who had so unexpectedly walked back into his life. Her appearing in his office the way she did had unnerved him. His simple little world had been rattled. And he kind of liked it.

None of that mattered if the hit man got to Emma. He needed to get his mind back on the mission: keeping Emma safe and solving the case. Once that was done, he could then maybe explore the feelings that kept trying to present themselves.

"One is never too old for happiness." Even as she said the words, he caught the sadness in her eyes.

"What about you? Have you ever been in love?" He asked the question but wasn't sure he really wanted the answer.

"Just once," Emma replied, looking out over the pond. "A long time ago."

"What happened?" He held his breath as he waited for her reply.

Emma shrugged and gave him a sad smile. "It wasn't meant to be."

Was she talking about him? He'd always thought he'd imagined the shock of attraction that had passed between them when they'd kissed. Maybe it had been real. They were both just so young then.

"Come on, I told you about Leslie." He bumped her shoulder with his.

She kicked at the dirt with her toe. "Let's just say I don't make good choices when it comes to love and relationships."

"I guess we still have a lot in common then."

"I guess."

Adam had no idea what to say next, so he said nothing. Instead he walked over to the edge of the pond and looked out over the water, wishing they could just go back in time about twelve years to a simpler life.

"Do you think it's safe to leave now?" Emma asked, breaking the tension that had settled in around them.

Adam checked his watch. It had been more than thirty minutes since the SUV had passed by. "I think so. We'll continue up the mountain and circle back around though, just in case he's pulled over somewhere waiting."

"Okay."

Once they were settled in the truck, Adam turned the vehicle around and headed down the dirt path toward the main road. As he eased out of their hiding place and onto the pavement, he hit the gas and sped up the incline. The road stayed empty.

"Let's get those little fur balls to the kennel, then I need to stop by the station to report the attack. Do you mind going with me?"

Emma glanced over at him. "That depends. You haven't told me where you plan to take me."

"I was planning to take you to a hotel, but I've since had a better idea."

"Oh? Where?"

He rolled the truck to a stop at an intersection and waited for the red light to turn green. "My uncle's cabin. The one by the pond we just left."

Emma frowned. "I'm not so sure that's the best idea."

"Actually, I think it's perfect. Totally off the grid, impossible to find, and I'd feel better leaving you there alone."

She shook her head. "No. I don't want to be alone. At least at a hotel there will be a lot of other people around. Harder for me to get killed with so many witnesses."

"Have you forgotten about the supermarket fiasco last night?" The light turned green and Adam made a right, heading back toward the center of town.

"Of course not!"

"So you know it doesn't matter how many people are around. If he finds you, he will kill you."

"Can't I just stay with you or at the station during the day and you can sleep at my house at night?"

Adam reached over and took her hand, giving it a little squeeze. "Emma, he knows where you live and has no issue showing up there."

She sighed. "I know. I don't really have much of a choice, do I?"

"I'm sorry. I know how hard this is." He turned off the main road on to a side street, pulling up in front of a gated yard. A white sign with black letters read Kellie's Kennels. "Is this the right place?"

"Yes." Emma reached for the door handle. "I'll be right back."

"I won't go anywhere," he said, giving her a wink and a smile.

Emma got out of the truck and pulled open the back door

to get the two dogs. "Come on, guys. Let's go play with Kellie."

She led the two dogs up the driveway. The door opened before she made it to the porch and a woman stepped outside, greeting Emma with a hug. The dogs jumped and yapped, obviously excited to see Kellie.

Good. That would make it easier for Emma to leave them for a few days. His phone chimed. He fished it out of his pocket and read the new message.

Waters: You coming in today or what?

Adam typed back a quick reply.

Adam: Be there soon. Ran into a little trouble on the way.

Waters: Everything good?

Adam: For now.

He typed his reply, then set the phone down in the center console.

Emma walked down the driveway, pulled open the passenger door, and climbed inside.

"They really seemed excited to see Kellie," Adam said as she buckled her seat belt.

"Kellie's amazing. Mom says she's got a real gift with animals."

Adam backed out of the driveway and headed toward the police station. The rest of their trip remained uneventful. Even as he parked in the fenced-in lot, he felt Emma relaxing. The last eighteen hours had been one adrenaline rush after another for her. She had to be hanging on by a thread at this point.

He parked his truck, jumped out, and jogged around to open Emma's door. Stepping in close, he placed his hands around her waist and lifted her down to the ground. Emma stumbled a little when her feet touched the ground, falling against his chest. Adam tightened his arms around her slightly, not wanting to let her go just yet.

Emma made no move to step back either. "I could have done that myself." He liked the way her cheeks turned pink and her breath caught as he reached up and tucked a strand of hair behind her ear.

He gave her a mock salute. "Just doing my job, miss. Adam Marshall, bodyguard, at your service."

"I'm pretty sure that none of this is in your job description." She placed her hands flat against his chest but didn't try to push him away.

"A Marshall man takes his duty very seriously." He grinned down at her, those soft pink lips of hers so tempting. Adam loosened his hold. "And right now, my sense of duty tells me to get you inside."

She reached out and took his hand, wrapping her long, slender fingers with his larger, thicker ones. "Just stay close, and I know I'll be okay."

"I'll always keep you safe, Emma."

***

The conviction in his words and the emotions in his eyes told Emma he meant what he said. Even as a high school athlete, Adam had always been very serious. His word had been his honor even then, and he did everything he could to be good and just and moral. Exactly why he made such a great police officer and why Miranda's death had hit him so hard.

They walked into the station without talking. He let go of her hand when they entered the building, holding the door for her.

"Emma? Seriously?" a familiar voice called to her from across the room.

"Carter!" Adam's youngest brother, dressed in full police gear, crossed the lobby in three long strides, scooped her up, and swung her in a circle.

"When did you get back to town?" He hugged her again as he set her on her feet. "Adam, look who it is!"

"Relax, little brother. I know. She came here with me."

"No!" Carter looked from Emma to Adam and back again. "You're the protective custody Adam's been on? Man, why didn't you call me?"

Adam gave his brother an annoyed look. "I had everything under control. Don't you need to get out on patrol?"

Carter laughed. "Give it a rest, dude. I'm headed out right now." He leaned in and pressed a kiss to Emma's cheek. "Welcome home, Em. Let's grab lunch one day."

She hugged him as Adam watched them, his face flushed. She had always loved pushing his buttons and by the looks of it, she was getting them all at once. "Sounds good to me."

"Don't you have somewhere to be, little brother?"

"I'm headed out now, *old* brother. Don't be getting your *Depends* all twisted up in a wad." Carter winked at Emma and left the precinct, whistling an unfamiliar tune. Emma watched the array of emotions that passed over Adam's expression as he stared after his brother.

"Do all the Marshall brothers work for the police department?"

Adam turned his attention back to her. "We're all in law enforcement. But only three of us work here; me, Carter and Jacob."

"Marshall! Just the man I wanted to see."

They both turned toward the booming voice. Adam stepped forward, his hand extended. "Agent Ryan. Good to see you. What can I do for you?"

Emma watched as the other man shoved his hands in his pockets instead of accepting Adam's greeting. A brief flash of some unidentified emotion passed over Adam's expression, but he showed no other reaction to the dismissal.

"Just came to touch base on the joint operation." He raised an eyebrow. "Don't want anyone dropping the ball on this one."

Adam nodded. "I think we are all on the same page here. Lieutenant Waters has been in touch with your boss, and we are all moving forward together."

Emma watched the volley of information pass between the two men as they shifted like two tigers eyeing each for a fight.

Agent Ryan looked at her. "New girlfriend?"

The way he said the words, laced with vitriol, made Emma's stomach turn.

Adam stepped to his left just enough that he stood between Emma and Agent Ryan. "An old friend that I am helping out with something."

"Are you sure she needs your kind of help?" Agent Ryan walked toward the door but stopped and turned to look at her.

"Watch your back with that one, Miss."

When he was gone, Emma turned to Adam. "Not your biggest fan, I assume?"

Adam shook his head. "That's the agent I mentioned last night. Unfortunately, he is the one assigned to this area from his field office so any cases that overlap, we are stuck with him. I guess he still carries a grudge."

Emma huffed. "He's a cocky jerk."

"Yeah." Adam motioned to the hall. "Shall we?"

"I need to run to the ladies' room quick," she said as they walked toward Adam's office.

"Remember where it is?"

"Yes. I'll meet you at your office in a minute, okay?" Emma had the sudden need for some space. All the adrenaline of the last twenty-four hours seemed to crash all at once, and tears lingered near the surface. The last thing she wanted was for Adam to see her cry again.

He nodded. She read the concern in his eyes and gave him a little smile before walking away down the hall. She'd barely made it into one of the stalls before the tears began to fall.

Closing the stall door, she leaned against it and let the tears run freely. All the stress of the last day or so poured out of her in the form of salty water. Emma hated to cry but this time she let it work itself out. It wasn't like she'd ever witnessed a murder or had someone trying to kill her before. When her tears ran dry, she grabbed a wad of toilet tissue, wiped at her eyes, and blew her nose.

Stepping out of the stall, she walked to the sink. Turning on the tap, she splashed cold water on her face in an attempt to quell some of the red puffiness around her eyes. With scratchy brown paper towel from a dispenser on the wall, she patted her face dry.

"Okay, girl. It's time to pull up your big girl panties and handle this. Adam can't protect you forever."

A loud rap on the door startled her.

"Emma? You okay?" Adam's muffled voice sounded worried.

She took a deep breath and opened the door. "I'm fine. Sorry, I didn't mean to worry you. Just needed a minute."

He looked her up and down, a small frown tugging at his lips. "Were you crying?"

"Maybe." She shrugged. "I cry when I'm stressed. It's a lousy trait I've been cursed with my entire life."

Adam wrapped an arm around her shoulders and led her to his office. Once the door was shut, he pulled her in close, and Emma let him. He ran a hand over her hair and then made small circles across her back.

"I know how scary this has been. I also know how strong you are. We're gonna solve this case and get these guys before they get to you." He lifted her chin with a finger so she was forced to look at him. "I promise, Emma."

"Don't make promises you might not be able to keep."

"I'm not." He let her go and stepped behind his desk.

"I just need to do a little paperwork, see my boss, and then I'll get you to my uncle's cabin. You'll be safe there."

"I want to go up the mountain with you. I need to see that place one more time."

Adam shook his head. "I don't think that's a good idea."

She narrowed her eyes at him. "Why not?"

Adam lightly stroked the stubble that grazed his chin. "Let's see—it's a crime scene? Someone tried to kill you there, not once but twice, and oh, it's a crime scene."

Emma pulled away and walked over to the windows. "But what about my story?"

"I'm afraid your story isn't the top priority here anymore, Em."

Emma dropped into a chair and folded her arms over her chest. "I *need* this, Adam."

He walked over to where she sat and squatted in front of her. "As much as I want to give you what you want, I also have policies and protocols I am bound by. Not to mention it is my responsibility to keep you safe and that is not the best way to do it. At all."

She frowned and huffed. "You always were a rule follower."

He shrugged. "Nothing wrong with that." Adam sat down at his desk and turned on his computer. "Let me take care of a couple things and then we'll head out. Are you hungry? We can grab lunch on the way."

"I could go for a burger and a shake. Maybe some hot and salty fries." Emma walked over and sat down in a chair by the window. She dug in her purse and pulled out her cell phone. "I'll wait here until you are ready. I have some messages to reply to."

They worked quietly for about twenty minutes before Adam pushed his chair back and stood up. "I'm going to meet with my boss for a few minutes and then we can head out."

"Okay. I need to make a call anyway."

Adam gave her his heart-stopping grin once more. He had begun to relax around her, slipping into the Adam she'd always known. "I won't be long. Promise."

That's what made her next move that much harder. When he left the room, Emma got up and followed. Peeking out around the corner of the doorframe, she watched as Adam disappeared into an office at the end of the hall. When the hall was empty, she stepped out of Adam's office and headed toward the lobby of the precinct. Luck totally had her back. The sergeant that had been manning the front desk was gone.

She strode across the small lobby and out the side door that led to the parking lot. She knew from riding with Adam the night before that the gate would open when she pushed the button, no security code needed to leave.

CHAPTER 10

Her poor little car with its busted-out window and newly-minted bullet hole accessories sat in the same spot where they had parked it the night before. Fishing her keys from her purse, Emma pulled open the door and slid in behind the wheel. The car complained for a moment and then started right up. She backed out of the spot, pulled up to the gate, and reached through her open window to push the Open button. As the gate slid aside, she pulled through and turned in the direction of the Blue Ridge Parkway. She needed to see that cabin once more by herself—

her entire career rested on her ability to find out who ran the drug traffic through Staunton. She just needed a few pictures of the cabin and the surrounding area. Of course, finding a nice pile of drugs in the middle of the room wouldn't hurt either. If she were being totally honest with herself, she had no idea what she hoped to find, it just needed to help her make the story.

Twenty minutes into the thirty-minute drive, her phone rang. She ignored it. It rang again. And again. Each time,

Adam's number showed up, and each time she kept on driving without answering the call. She now had only a twenty-minute head start that would shrink quickly once she had to hike up that mountain.

Her phone rang again.

Emma hit the gas and drove faster.

When she made it to the mountain, she parked her car at the adjacent rest area. Moving as quickly as she could, Emma navigated the tangled brush. Halfway up the trail, a fat squirrel ran across the path in front of her and into a brushy area, sending a flock of birds up into the air. One of the birds flew in so close, it caught in her hair. Emma slapped at it, trying not to squeal or make noise. Finally, it freed itself and she trudged on. She made good time, reaching the edge of the clearing in almost half the time it had taken her the day before.

The sun burned hot as she tucked a few stray hairs behind her ears and wiped some sweat from her forehead. It had to be close to noon. Even so late in the fall, the sun still gave off a good amount of heat. Too bad she didn't think to look for the access road the murderer had taken. Or, maybe it was a good thing. She'd have no means to get away if they returned and blocked her vehicle.

Emma practically tiptoed across the small clearing. When she made it to the same little window where she'd witnessed the murder, she peered through the layers of grime at the dim interior. The cabin looked empty, so she slowly worked her way around to the front porch. The door stood slightly ajar, with four or five different sets of shoe prints in the dirt and dust. Emma grabbed her phone and snapped a couple photos of each of the different patterns.

A quick check of the time told her Adam would be there soon. She had to move quickly.

Standing to one side of the door, Emma sucked in a breath and kicked lightly at the base of it to push it all the way open. When no rain of gunfire greeted the motion, Emma stepped through the door and into the cabin. The chair the dead man had sat in now stood in the kitchen area. The pool of blood had dried into a dark stain, and a cabinet above the counter had been left open. Careful to stay along the edge of the room and not touch anything, Emma walked over and stepped up on a rickety foot stool. Turning the flashlight on her cell phone on, she peered inside the cupboard. A few rusty cans of soup and chili littered the otherwise empty space. The only thing missing was dust. The light glinted off something in the corner of the top shelf. Stretching, she aimed her phone at it and took a quick picture.

Emma stepped down off the stool and grabbed a dusty wooden spoon out of a canister by the stove. Climbing back up, she used it to move the object toward her. Pulling her sleeve over her hand, she knocked it into her palm and studied her find. In her palm sat a shiny gold ring with a black stone in the center. Rolling it over with the spoon she found the initials KP, a heart, and the name Tara inscribed on the inside.

A board on the front porch creaked. Emma froze. Another creak sounded. Dropping the ring back inside the cabinet, she stepped off the stool and looked frantically around the tiny cabin for a place to hide. A narrow door in the corner of the kitchen area caught her eye. Emma crossed the small space as quietly as she could and pulled the door open to find a tiny utility closet.

Squeezing in beside an old mop and broom, she prayed that there were no spiders in the maze of webs attached to them. Emma pulled the door closed and listened. Heavy footsteps moved slowly across the room. They stopped moving at about the center of the space, as best she could tell. Practically holding her breath, Emma waited to see what the person would do next.

Something ran across the toe of her shoe. Emma jumped and tried not to make a sound, but a little squeak of terror snuck out.

The footsteps started again, moving closer to her hiding place. Emma stepped back, shrinking herself as much as she could to get to the back of the closet. The person paused. She held her breath. A full minute later, the footsteps began again.

Whatever shared the closet with her grabbed her pant leg and started to climb. This time, Emma screamed and burst out of the closet.

"Get off me!" She caught sight of a rat clinging to her jeans and started jumping and kicking. The critter let her go and scurried away.

Emma froze when she realized what she'd done. Without looking around, she took off for the front door. Strong arms grabbed her and wrapped around her chest.

"Let me go!" She pulled at the arms that held her.

"Emma! It's me!" A familiar voice spoke in low tones next to her ear.

Emma stopped struggling and turned to look at her captor. "Adam."

"Yes." He let her go.

"Why didn't you say anything when you came in the cabin?" She shivered. "I was in that closet with a rat and God only knows what else."

Adam shrugged. "I didn't know for sure if you were here. Or who else might be. You know, since I told you to stay away."

She put her hands on her hips and gave him her best annoyed look. "You knew exactly where I was. You called me at least a dozen times."

***

Adam stared at the woman in front of him, holding back the laughter that he knew would make her even madder. Anger made her even more adorable. "I didn't know you were here. You didn't answer any of those calls, remember?"

The anger faded quickly, and she waved a hand in the air, dismissing him. "Whatever. You still didn't have to be so—cop-like."

This time he did laugh. "I'll try to remember next time."

"None of this is funny."

"You're right, it's not. You contaminated the entire scene."

She shrugged. "I just wanted a few minutes alone. Before you turned it into a crime scene and didn't let me in here anymore."

"It's already a crime scene and like I said, you have now contaminated it."

Emma scowled. "I didn't touch anything except that wooden spoon." She pointed at the utensil lying on the floor.

Adam shook his head and sighed. "You shouldn't have even come in here. What if it had been the killer and not me that found you?"

Emma walked over to the front door and peered outside, speaking with her back to him. "I didn't think that far ahead. I just wanted one last look around. See if there was anything that would help my story before you totally took over."

Adam walked over to where she stood and rested his hands on her shoulders. "All that matters now is your safety. Not a story. Not a drug case. We have to keep you safe. Okay, so the case matters but the story isn't yours to tell anymore. As soon as you became a material witness, that cancelled everything else."

She turned to look at him over her shoulder. "What does that matter? If you don't solve the case, I'll have to live in the Marshall safe house for the rest of my life."

He smiled. "The Marshall safe house? It's just an old fishing cabin that happens to be hidden and off the grid."

Emma pointed out the door. "Do you hear that?"

They both listened for a second before Adam spoke. "Sounds like a car. Was there a car here the last time you were here alone?"

"Yes. A dark sedan." The sound got louder as the car got closer. "There is a dirt road that leads up here from another part of the mountain."

"We need to get out of here." Adam took her hand and led her out the door. They sprinted across the field and into the trees.

"Do you think it's the killer?" Emma whispered as they moved to a place where they could watch the front door.

"I don't know. Maybe."

As they waited, a black SUV pulled up in front of the cabin. One of the headlights had been smashed and the front bumper sported a large dent.

"Look at the front of that truck," Emma whispered.

"Yeah. I know."

Two men climbed out of the truck. One went to the door of the cabin and the other to the back of the SUV. Emma looked at him, and Adam shook his head. He had no idea who it was either.

The second man opened the back of the truck and messed with something in there, then closed it up again. The first man had already gone inside, so he followed suit and disappeared in the cabin as well.

Adam strained to hear any sounds inside the tiny house but couldn't make out a single one. Then, as quickly as they disappeared, they reappeared on the front porch.

"I'm positive I dropped it in there. Tara is gonna kill me. Or worse." The first man fidgeted with the ring finger of his right hand.

"Dude, you dragged me all the way back up here for a piece of costume junk. You know the boss doesn't like anyone coming up here unless he tells them to. He doesn't want the drop man to know who his guys are." The other man kicked at an empty soda can that sat on the floor of the porch. "Come on, Kirk. Let's get out of here before he figures it out."

"What does it matter? This place ain't a secret anymore, thanks to Rudy."

"Once Rudy takes care of that woman, things will get right back to normal. Now, let's get out of here before someone sees us."

"It sure is taking him a long time. Maybe Rudy's losing his touch." The man called Kirk frowned. "I'm telling you, Marco, if she finds out I lost it—I'd rather face the boss."

"So, don't tell her. Go buy another one before she notices."

Kirk exhaled heavily. "Yeah. I guess." He walked over to the passenger side of the truck and climbed into the front seat.

His buddy, Marco, kicked the can one more time and then went over and got into the driver seat. The engine roared to life as Marco turned the truck around and headed back down the mountain.

"I wonder what he was looking for?" Adam said.

Emma looked over at him. "I think I know."

"How?" Her admission surprised him.

"Because I think I found it first."

He looked down to see Emma holding out her phone. A picture of her sleeve-covered palm holding a gold ring with a black stone. "How do you know this is his?"

She scrolled to the next photo and pointed to an inscription.

"Because it has a heart and the name Tara inscribed on the back."

"Where did you find that? Better yet, where is it now?"

"I found it in the cabinet over the stove. I think that might be the drop place. There wasn't any dust in there. Like, at all."

"Well, he obviously didn't find it. Can you show me where it's at?"

Emma nodded and led the way back to the cabin. When they stepped inside, she pointed to the cabinet. "There. I found it way in the back corner."

Adam stepped up onto the step stool and pulled a flashlight from his pocket that he shone inside the cupboard. "You're right. There's definitely not much dust in here, except on the old cans of food. It looks like someone dragged something though, leaving some scratch marks in the wood." He reached in a pocket and grabbed a plastic baggie. Using the bag like a glove he picked up the ring and wrapped the bag around it before tucking it in his shirt pocket.

Adam stepped down off the chair and returned the flashlight to his pocket. "I think you might be right. This has to be the drop spot."

"So, what do we do now?" Emma asked.

"I'm going to call it in so that the scene can be secured and the techs can check for more evidence. Now that I know there's actually been a crime committed here, we need to follow procedure."

"If you do that, you'll never make your case. They won't come here anymore."

"Let me call the lieutenant and see what he thinks." Adam stepped away to place his call. While it rang, he watched Emma's expression run through a full gamut of emotion, wondering about the secrets he had really begun to suspect she carried around with her.

When he explained the situation to Lieutenant Waters, his boss agreed with not turning it into an official scene yet. He'd send someone up to watch it, out of sight, until a sting could be set up. Adam just had to take plenty of photos and bring back a sample of the bloodstain. Easy enough to accomplish by pulling a couple of splinters out of the floorboards.

Putting his phone in his pocket, he walked back to the front of the cabin. "I just have to take a few photos and then we can head out."

Emma frowned. "Lockdown time."

Adam's stomach made a loud growling sound. "We get lunch first though. I'm starving, and you promised me a burger and hot, salty fries."

She laughed. "Fine. But then what?"

Adam rested a hand at the small of Emma's back and led her toward the porch. He wondered for a moment if the touch was too intimate, but Emma showed no discomfort, and if he were being honest, it just felt right. "I'll get you settled at the cabin, then head back to the station to set up surveillance on this place. We need to catch them in the act."

"How?" she asked as they crossed the clearing.

"I'm part of a joint operation with the FBI and ATF. We've long suspected they had a drop spot in the area, and you have cracked that part of the case for us. We still need to catch them in the act though and you were right, if we tape off the cabin and bring crime scene in here, we lose all the ground we've gained. There's a lot of man hours invested in this. I'm going to work out a rotation for each agency, make sure the cabin is being watched twenty-four-seven until we get what we need."

"And I get to stay locked up in the middle of nowhere, missing all the fun." Adam took his photos and collected the splinters before exiting the cabin.

Emma stayed quiet as they followed the path down the mountain. Adam gave her some space to work through the emotions she had to be feeling about everything that had happened. When they made it to the spot where they had both left their cars, Emma went straight to hers without speaking to him.

"Emma?" he called after her.

"I know. It's time for me to go to prison." She didn't even look back at him. "I'll follow you to the station so we can park my car."

CHAPTER 11

Emma was frustrated, and he didn't blame her one bit. The whole situation had so many ifs, ands, and buts—too much uncertainty for his type A brain to accept. The one thing he did know though, was that he had to get Emma to safety so he could concentrate on finding the people running drugs through that cabin and the person who wanted Emma dead. Not to mention, he really needed to locate the murder victim Emma had seen the day before. Until they did, no body meant no victim, and in the eyes of the court, it would be hard to prove a crime.

But first, they needed food.

Adam walked over to her car and tapped on the glass. Emma put the window down. "What?"

"When we get back to the station, I need to put the cuff link and the blood samples in the evidence room. We can also leave your car in the secure lot again. Then, of course, we'll eat."

Emma rolled her eyes and motioned to the car. "I doubt anyone is gonna try and steal this hot mess."

"It's not that bad," Adam said.

"Whatever you say. I'll follow you to the station."

"Sounds good." Adam got into his own vehicle and pulled out of the lot.

The drive to the station passed uneventfully. Emma followed him into the lot and parked her car in the back corner. She didn't say much as they walked inside.

Adam pointed to a sofa in the lobby. "If you want to wait here, I'll only be a minute."

Emma nodded and sat as he walked down a hall toward the property and evidence room. Her new round of silence worried him.

"Hey, Marshall." One of the patrol officers, John Parrish, stood at a table filling out an evidence form for a shotgun and some heroin.

"Busy day?" Adam motioned to the items as he grabbed a blank form and an envelope.

"Nothing out of the ordinary." Parrish used a zip tie to attach a tag to the shotgun.

"I remember a day when guns and drugs weren't part of the daily life in Staunton."

Parrish elbowed him in the side. "Old Man Marshall talkin' about the good ole days."

"Watch who you're calling old." Adam dropped the ring in the envelope, sealed it, and put secure evidence tape over the flap.

"Did you see the hottie that was in here this morning?" Parrish opened one of the gun lockers in the evidence room and placed the shotgun inside.

"What hottie?" He better not have been referring to Emma.

"Brunette with a killer body. Lieutenant says she's in protective custody. I wonder who the lucky guy is that gets to protect her. I'd be willing to protect her all day long. All night too."

Adam narrowed his eyes and gave Parrish a glare. "Don't talk about women like they're objects. How would you feel if someone talked about your sister or your mama that way?"

Parrish raised his hands in mock surrender. "Whoa, old man. I'm just saying she was fine."

"You're right. She is fine. She has a mind of her own, a quick wit, and she's smarter than you and me put together."

"You dating her or something?" Parrish placed the bag of marijuana in a paper evidence bag with secure tape holding it closed. The other man meant it as a joke but Adam took it as anything but.

"We're old friends. And I'd appreciate it if you showed her and all women a little more respect."

Parrish laughed. "Oh, Marshall, you really are an old man."

Adam filed his forms and locked up the envelopes in the evidence room. "If showing respect to other humans makes me old, then so be it, but I don't know when thirty-two classified as old." He slammed the drawer to the file cabinet. "Be safe out there."

As he walked away, he could feel Parrish's eyes on him. Maybe he had gotten a little worked up, but so many of the new kids joining the force seemed to lack basic compassion and manners. Or he really was just getting old.

Emma still sat on the same little couch when he returned to the lobby. "You ready to eat?"

She nodded and stood up. "Is this like a death row prisoner getting their last meal?"

Adam laughed. "What's that supposed to mean?"

"I'm about to be locked away for an indefinite amount of time." Emma pushed the door open and walked out of the station.

He stopped walking. "And you think I won't feed you?"

She looked back at him. "You know that's not what I meant."

Adam started walking again, catching up with her. "I gotta admit, Emma, I'm sensing a lot of hostility and I have absolutely no idea why."

She sighed heavily. "I know. I'm sorry. This whole thing, not being able to go where I want and do what I want, is hard. I've been on my own for a really long time, coming and going as I please. Now, we're talking about locking me away for who knows how long."

Adam unlocked his truck and opened the passenger door for Emma. "It's not like you're going to prison."

"Might as well be." Emma climbed up into the cab of the truck. "Don't worry. I'll get over it. I'm just complaining."

He stepped into the space between the truck and the door, standing so close to Emma he could feel her warmth. Reaching up, he ran the tips of his fingers along the line of her jaw.

"I have to keep you safe, Emma. This is the only way I know how."

Emma wrapped her fingers around his wrist, moving his hand to her lips. She pressed a kiss to his knuckles. "I'm not Leslie. You can't bring her back by obsessing over this."

Her words cut straight through his soul, releasing all the pain and memories he'd carefully stored away. He swallowed hard against the emotions. "It's not about Leslie. Or, even Miranda, if that's what you're thinking. It's about keeping you alive. I've lost enough people I care about."

She pressed a palm to his cheek. Her touch sent his heart racing in his chest. "I know. First Miranda and then Leslie. I'm sorry I dumped all of this on you."

Adam shook his head. "You didn't dump anything on me." His stomach let out a loud complaint. It had been much too long since his last meal. "How about we get that lunch and have a long talk about everything later? I think we both have things we need to discuss."

Emma gave him an odd look but nodded and pulled her seat belt over her shoulder.

"About the case, I mean," Adam said quickly, closing the truck door. He jogged around the back of the truck, taking a moment to get his emotions in check.

Emma was right about one thing, and he definitely didn't want to admit it, even to himself. He had been reliving Leslie's last few minutes over and over since Emma had shown up in his office. He couldn't have done anything to prevent Leslie's—or Miranda's—death but he could prevent Emma's. If only she'd stop fighting him at every turn. He climbed into the truck and shut the door.

"I was thinking we'd hit up Pop's Diner for lunch. He's got the best fries in Staunton." Adam turned the key and the engine roared to life.

"Sounds like a plan." Emma gripped the door handle as the truck moved. "I haven't seen my uncle in a while."

Adam pointed to her hand and laughed. "I'm not that bad of a driver."

"It's habit. Sorry." Emma moved her hand to her lap.

"I can't imagine who you've been riding with." Adam pulled out of the lot and onto the main street of town. His stomach growled loudly, again.

Emma nodded toward Adam. "Time to feed the monster?"

"No better place than Pop's." He pulled the truck to a stop at a red light. Down the block, he caught sight of a familiar vehicle. Black with darkly tinted windows. He pointed through the windshield. "I think someone's looking for us."

Emma let out a long breath. "Can't we even get some food without someone trying to kill me? What do we do now?"

"Hold on. I have an idea." Adam flipped a U-turn in the middle of the street and headed back to the precinct. "I don't know why I didn't think of this before."

"Think of what?"

"The killer knows my truck. He knows your car. But if I take one of the marked cars, he won't recognize us. At least not right away."

Emma nodded. "Good idea." Her stomach let out a growl almost as loud as his had. "Because I think I really need to eat soon."

Adam pulled the truck up to the gate and punched in the code. As it slid to the side, he drove into the lot and parked beside a SUV with the city markings on it. "Hang out here while I run inside and grab the keys." He pushed open the door and jumped out of the cab.

Emma gave him a mock salute. "Yes, sir, officer, sir."

He paused. "Sorry. I guess I slipped into cop mode for a minute there."

She smiled at him. "It's okay. I couldn't resist the tease, that's all."

Adam winked at her and closed the door, his stomach rumbling once more. As he walked into the police station, he took one last quick look over his shoulder. Emma sat in the front seat, looking at her phone, her silky hair falling around her face. The sun caught some of the natural golden highlights, forming a halo-like aura around her head. His heart rate kicked up a notch once more as he imagined pushing that hair behind her ear and pressing a kiss to the sensitive spot on the side of her neck.

He shook his head to clear the image. They had to solve this case before anything more could happen. Not that he was entirely sure anything more would happen. He and Emma had a considerable amount of water under their bridge, and he had no idea if she was willing to wade through it with him or not.

* * *

Emma pulled out her phone, opened her email, and scanned the new messages. The feeling like she was being watched gave her a run of goose bumps on her arms. As she glanced up, she caught Adam looking at her. The intensity in his stare warmed her cheeks, and she looked away quickly. Seeing him again, spending so much time together under such crazy circumstances, had her head and her heart all confused. Adam had been her first crush. She'd just never told anyone, and she'd wanted him to kiss her that night, despite knowing her best friend's intentions.

Emma turned her focus back to her phone. There were several unread emails that needed her attention, and right now was not the time to get distracted by old feelings.

There was a message from her parents. She opened that one to see several pictures of them on a beach in Fiji. Her mom had the biggest smile Emma had ever seen. Their trip was definitely the right way for her hardworking parents to spend their retirement. A third email came from an unknown sender. Emma got a lot of spam email and letters from readers. Most of those were comments and questions on the articles she wrote. A few were from angry readers and the occasional wannabe stalker. She almost deleted it but at the last second changed her mind and opened it.

Miss Thomas,

We know where you live. We know everything about you. You can run but you can't hide.

There was no signature, and the email address gave her no information about the sender.

Adam walked out of the building. Emma grabbed her

purse and phone and climbed down out of the truck before Adam could do something like help her down again.

His smile faded when he got to where she stood. "Are you okay?"

"I am. But I have to show you something." She opened the email and handed her phone to Adam so he could read it.

He frowned, two little creases forming at the bridge of his nose. For the briefest second, Emma wanted to reach up and touch those lines, but she didn't.

"When did you get this?" he asked.

Emma shrugged. "Sometime since we left the house this morning. Timestamp says nine thirty."

"Please forward it to me so I can get someone to try and track it." Adam handed her a business card with his work email address on it.

Emma tapped out the address and hit Send. Adam's phone pinged a moment later.

"Let's get you something to eat and then out to the cabin. I'll feel better when you're out of harm's way. Then I can find this creep and put a stop to all this." Adam pulled open the door to the police SUV. His expression had turned serious, determination darkening his eyes. The smile she'd been enjoying so much that morning had been replaced by lips set in a straight line.

Emma climbed into the SUV and waited while Adam put her overnight bag and computer case in the back. When he got in the truck beside her, he inserted the key and started the engine before speaking again. "How do you feel about a drive-through rather than sitting down at the diner?"

"Nope. I want a meal. If it's going to be my last, it needs to have more flavor than fryer oil and dehydrated onions." Emma crossed her arms over her chest and gave him a look that said she wasn't budging on that.

Adam sighed. "Fine. We'll go to the diner but stay away from doors and windows while we're in there."

She reached over and touched his arm lightly, hoping she didn't react visibly when the spark of energy bounced between them at the simple contact. "Thank you, Adam."

"It's just lunch." He reached up and placed his hand on top of hers.

"I'm not talking just about lunch, and I'm pretty sure you know that."

"Yeah. I do. I'd do anything for you. I think you know that—have always known that."

Emma moved her hand away and turned to look out the window. They both stayed quiet for the rest of the drive.

When they reached the diner, the parking lot was full. Adam parked the SUV beside two other Staunton police cars and turned it off. "I figure this gives us another layer of cover. Anyone comes driving by, they will just see three police vehicles."

"Good idea." Emma grabbed the handle and started to open the truck.

"Wait," Adam said. "Let me come around and clear the area first. I want to be able to cover you if he suddenly shows up."

Emma pulled the door closed and waited as Adam checked the parking lot and the road that ran in front of the diner. He walked around the SUV and positioned himself between her and the road as he pulled the door open.

"You ready?"

His smile had returned, and that made Emma smile too.

"I've been ready for hours." Her stomach let out a loud growl, making them both laugh.

Adam stayed beside her on their way into the diner, one hand pressed lightly to her lower back and the other resting on the pistol slung at his hip. When they entered the restaurant, he kept her in front of him.

"Emma!" An older man wearing a stained apron appeared in the entry from the kitchen.

"Uncle Marlon!" She rushed forward to give the man a hug and a peck on the cheek, forgetting that Adam was trying to block her from view outside the diner.

"It's so good to see you, little one!" He placed his hands on her cheeks briefly, then moved them to her shoulders. "You've been gone too long. You're much too thin! Don't they have food in Richmond?"

Emma let the laughter flow. Her uncle's joy in life had always been infectious, and this time was no exception. "Of course they do, Uncle! But they also have twenty-four-hour-a-day gyms."

Uncle Marlon shook his head. "You need to eat. I'll feed you. And your friend." He motioned to Adam.

"Don't you remember Adam Marshall?" Emma asked.

"Of course I do! He and the other policemen eat here regularly. It's just been a really long time since you two have been in here together."

Adam stepped forward and shook the older man's hand. "It's good to see you again, sir. Emma here is actually helping me out with a little police business. But she just had to see her favorite uncle too."

Marlon smiled, a broad, toothy grin. "Excellent! You can sit anywhere you like."

"Thank you, sir." Adam started to direct her toward a table in the rear of the space with no close windows.

"No salad!" Marlon called after them. "You eat a cheeseburger! And double fries. You're too skinny!"

"Yes, Uncle Marlon! You keep saying that," Emma called back.

"Because it's true!"

"Your uncle always thinks everyone is too thin." Clara James, a longtime resident of Staunton, touched Emma on the arm as they passed. "He gave me a cheeseburger and double fries also."

"Ms. Clara! It's so nice to see you!" Emma stopped and gave the older woman a hug. "You look wonderful. How's that new little grandbaby of yours?"

"Looks just like his daddy, Logan." Clara picked up her cell phone and pulled up a photo of a blonde-haired, blue-eyed cherub. "Poor Angie, it's like she didn't even contribute. Not a sign of her beautiful Italian heritage anywhere in this boy."

"How are the twins?" Adam asked, shifting their positions so he blocked Emma from view of the window. Clara's sons Kaiden and Keegan had graduated with Adam and Emma. They'd gone into federal law enforcement.

"Oh, you know. Doing their lawman thing out at the beach. It's still my hope they will one day move closer to home."

"I'm sure they will." Emma patted the woman on the arm. "Please tell them we said hello, and our congratulations to Logan and his wife."

"I will, dear. Thank you so much. It was wonderful to see you again. Together, like the old days."

When they reached the back booth, Emma slid into the seat that faced the rest of the diner, expecting Adam to sit across from her. Instead, he settled in beside her, grinning. "Don't you remember? A cop never has his back to the door."

His denim-clad thigh brushed against hers, sending a little rush of warmth through her. She wondered if he felt it too. Adam scanned the diner twice before leaning back against the booth. He let his arm lie casually along the back of the vinyl seat. They'd sat that way a hundred times as teenagers, but this time Emma was hyperaware of how close he was.

"I guess it's been a while since I've had to think about it."

"Your uncle is a good man." Adam picked up his fork and twirled it in his fingers slowly. "He always supports the department and our officers."

"His father, Marlon senior, was chief of police here once upon a time."

"Really?" The surprise in his expression was genuine. "I had no idea. Marlon never mentioned it."

"He was killed in the line of duty. Mom says he rarely talks about it, since he was just a toddler when it happened."

"He's your mother's brother?" Adam asked. "I didn't realize that."

"No. He married Mom's oldest sister, Hillary. Remember, Mom is the youngest of ten." Emma laughed.

Marlon appeared then, followed by a young girl in a black apron. He placed plates of burgers and fries in front of Emma and Adam. The girl gave them each a chocolate milkshake. Marlon grinned. "I didn't wait for you to order. You need to eat, little girl."

"Thanks, Uncle Marlon. This is exactly what I've been dreaming about all morning." Emma gave the older man a big smile. His already ruddy cheeks darkened with her compliment.

Adam removed his arm from behind her, and Emma felt the absence of his nearness immediately. She pushed away the urge to move in closer to him and focused instead on her uncle and the tantalizing food he'd placed in front of her.

"Eat!" Marlon waved a hand and walked away with the young waitress in tow.

Emma picked up her burger and took a huge bite. "Mmm... this is so good."

Adam did the same and nodded his agreement. "Best burger in the entire Blue Ridge Mountains."

Picking up a few fries and dipping them in ketchup, Emma casually said, "Speaking of the mountains—"

Adam raised a hand to stop her. "I need to get you to the cabin, Emma. I have to try and figure out who wants you dead so I can stop them."

She leaned back against the booth. "I could just stay with you."

"It would be too distracting."

Emma frowned and slid away from Adam. "Gee, thanks."

Turning in his seat, Adam took her hand in his. He ran his thumb lightly across the inside of her wrist, sending little shock waves through her. "I didn't mean it like that. I can't focus on finding the man who wants you dead if I am more worried about keeping you safe. At least out at the cabin, I know you will be okay. Especially if I can talk one or more of my brothers into staying there with you."

Emma looked down at their joined hands. He'd held her hand so many times over the years, and she'd never thought twice about it. But now, it looked like their hands were always meant to be together. If she died, or worse, if something happened to Adam trying to protect her... She couldn't even finish that thought.

She sighed. "Fine. I'll go to the cabin, but promise me you will be back tonight?"

Adam grinned. "I promise. Now let's eat before all this deliciousness gets cold."

Smiling back at him, Emma nodded. "I am half starved."

As they sat and ate, side by side like they'd done so many times before, Emma almost forgot about Miranda, the man that wanted her dead, and everything else that had happened since the last time they'd eaten a burger together.

CHAPTER 12

An hour later, they pulled up in front of the little cabin hidden deep in the woods. It had a small covered front porch with an old rocking chair in one corner. Next to the door sat a faded red cooler. On top of that, a dented bait can lay on its side. Propped in a corner were three or four fishing poles. A giant, mounted fish of some sort hung over the door.

Emma pointed to the fish. "You weren't kidding. This really is a fishing cabin."

Adam chuckled. "Yeah. It really is. Let's go inside, and I'll show you around."

"Please tell me it has running water? I'm not much of an outhouse kinda gal."

He pulled her bags from the back of the SUV and led her to the porch. "Yes, it has running water. But it's a well, so you have to conserve. No hour-long showers or anything like that."

"Oh, thank goodness. I can handle the short shower in exchange for the flushing toilet."

"I guess camping probably isn't your thing." Adam set her

things down and reached up to the giant fish over the door, pulling a key out of its mouth. After unlocking the door, he replaced the key, pushed the door open, and motioned for her to enter.

She laughed. "Not really. Unless you mean in an RV or a hotel room. I can work with either of those."

Emma wasn't sure what she had expected but it wasn't what she saw. Hardwood floors polished to a high shine greeted her first. As she glanced around the space, taking in the muted earth tones of the décor, granite counters, sink in the kitchenette, and a large flat-screen television hanging on the far wall, she sucked in a breath. "Wow. Not at all what I thought."

"Uncle Walt likes things a certain way, even when he's escaping Aunt Jane for the weekend."

"This is amazing. From outside it looks worn out and dusty. On the inside, it's practically professionally decorated."

"It is professionally decorated, actually." Adam crossed the room to where two closed doors stood, side by side. He stopped at the first door. "This is the bathroom."

Emma pushed the door open and walked into the small space. A completely tiled walk-in shower was the first thing she saw, followed by the granite sink with its gorgeous fixtures. "Wow. This is beautiful. I know I keep saying it, but—wow."

She looked back at Adam to see him smiling at her, still standing in the doorway. There was an unfamiliar look in his eyes as he watched her walk around the bathroom, admiring all the details. "Wait until you see the bedroom." He motioned toward the other closed door.

"Okay." She walked out of the bathroom and over to the bedroom door. Opening it, her mouth literally fell open in surprise. "This is phenomenal."

The queen-sized four-poster bed was wrapped in layers of white mesh, forming a curtain around it. A comforter on the bed was a blend of blues and grays and lavenders, unlike the earth tones she'd seen in the rest of the house. Soft gray paint covered the walls. A long dresser with a simple mirror ran down one wall, and a nightstand stood by one side of the bed, a small lamp and a digital clock resting on it.

Emma walked into the room and turned in a slow circle. "I don't even know what to say. I don't understand how this can be so beautiful on the inside and so—old on the outside."

Adam set her bags on the dresser. "You can have this room. I'll bunk on the sofa."

She shook her head. "Oh, no! I couldn't do that. You sleep in the bed. I can sleep out there."

"It's fine. Really. I've fallen asleep on that sofa so many times it's like a second bed to me. Plus, I can watch Sports Center until I pass out."

"Still the world's biggest football fan, I see." Emma set her purse on the dresser with her other things.

"You can take the man out of the game but you can never fully take the game out of the man."

Emma turned and found herself locked in between the dresser and Adam's broad chest. She reached up and fiddled with one of the buttons on his henley. "This is the first time we've ever been in a bedroom together without one of us having to sneak in through a window."

Adam rested his hands on the dresser on either side of her. "Those nights were some of the best of my life. Lying next to you, talking about our hopes and dreams. I miss those days. I was so lonely when you left for college."

Surprising herself, Emma wrapped her arms around his waist and rested her ear against his chest. She felt the beat of his heart as it fell in sync with her own. "I couldn't stay here, Adam. Miranda's death—it was all too much." Not that things had been any better in Richmond the last few months or so.

He kissed the top of her hair. "I know. I have some things to say about that too. Later. After I take care of the case."

Emma nodded. "Okay."

Adam stepped back and turned away from her. She caught him adjusting his jeans as he walked from the room. That secretly pleased her as she followed him to the main living area.

"I'm going to head out now. There's a fully stocked pantry and fridge. Should have everything you need. I'll be back by dinnertime." He strode toward the door, car keys in hand.

Emma followed him. "That's it? You're just going to leave right now."

Adam turned around, his expression serious. "You don't want to be stuck out here forever, do you?"

Emma looked around the small, lush cabin. "I don't

know, it might not be so bad after all. Is there Wi-Fi?"

He raised an eyebrow and gave her half a smile. "Of course. I'll be back in a couple of hours. I'm going to work on setting up surveillance on the cabin for the next couple of nights. That takes some arranging to make happen."

"I want to go with you for that."

"No, Emma. It could be dangerous if someone shows up."

She stepped back, forcing Adam to let her go. "I want to be there. Please?"

"Can we talk about it tonight? I really need to get back to the precinct."

"Nice move, Adam Marshall. Deflection and postponement." Emma narrowed her eyes at him. "Don't forget to come back here."

He reached up and tucked a piece of hair behind her ear, letting his fingertips trail the line of her chin lightly. His eyes had become dark, swirling pools of emotion that drew her in and held her gaze. "How could I forget now that you are finally here again?"

Without another word, Adam turned and walked out of the cabin. She barely heard the latch click over the sound of her heart beating in her chest. Adam's last words lingered in the air around her. His eyes and his words had just said so much. Running her own fingers along the same path Adam's had followed, she swallowed hard against the rage of emotion threatening to break free.

He'd missed her. He'd thought about her over the years. He'd wanted her to be here in Staunton with him.

* * *

Adam forced his mind to focus on the mission at hand. If he didn't get out of those woods and back to the station soon, he'd forget what needed to be done and go back to Emma. He hated leaving her alone when there was so much he wanted—no, *needed* to tell her. So many words left unsaid for so long. And now, under the pressure of her life being in danger and running on pure adrenaline just didn't seem like the right time to pour out all his emotions to her.

He'd spent what felt like a lifetime regretting that night; not forgiving himself for his part in the tragedy of Miranda's death. Emma leaving Staunton had made it easy for him to ignore it most days. Except when he passed the church he'd attended as a youth and guilt sucker-punched him in the gut. That he regretted even more than his part in their friend's death—not going after Emma and telling her how he felt. If he had, maybe none of the stuff with Leslie would have happened. She'd be alive, her parents wouldn't hate him, and he wouldn't carry the guilt of the deaths of two women in his life.

Once he solved this case and found her wannabe killer, he and Emma could have a long overdue talk about all those feelings he'd kept locked away for over a decade.

For now, though, his only concern had to be Emma's safety.

As he passed the turn for the Blue Ridge Turnpike, he decided not to go to the station after all. Pulling an illegal U-turn in the middle of the street, he hit the gas and headed back to the mountain and the cabin that sat at the center of everything. His case. The murder Emma had witnessed. And the man who wanted her dead.

He considered looking for the access road and driving up the mountain, but on the off chance someone else might be there, he opted to hike back up. Parking his SUV in the same lot as usual, he locked the police vehicle and began the climb up the mountain. Alone, he moved quickly, pushing through brush and brambles along the path that he and Emma had forged over the last couple of days.

When he reached the clearing, he'd already broken out in a sweat over every inch of his body despite the cool fall air. Ignoring the salty water running down his forehead, he crossed the clearing to the cabin and peeked in the side window. The place looked as empty as it had earlier. Following the wall of the cabin to the small covered porch, he pulled on some gloves he'd had in his pocket and turned the knob of the front door.

He had no idea what he expected to find that he hadn't already seen that morning. His gut told him there was something he'd missed, and his gut instincts rarely steered him wrong.

It didn't look like anyone else had been there since he and Emma and the two men had. Starting to the right of the door and moving slowly, he searched every inch of wall, floor, and ceiling for something that would help him. It wasn't until he reached an old shelf along the north-facing wall that he hit the jackpot. A couple of dusty books, an empty flower vase, and a small statue of a grizzly bear sat on the shelf. The books hadn't been touched in years, and the vase was filled with cobwebs. The bear statue, however, had no dust or grime and seemed almost brand-new. In fact, when he picked it up, he found a price tag still attached to the bottom from a local shop. Turning it around, he inspected the bear from all angles until he found exactly what he had been looking for.

A tiny camera, fitted into one of the eyes, and a small switch that sat beneath its tail. When he pushed on it, a tiny little memory card sprung out of the statue's bottom.

"Gotcha now." Adam tucked the memory card in his pocket and replaced the bear exactly where he had found it, aimed right at the spot where the shooting had occurred.

After poking around a little bit more, he headed back to the truck. He'd get one of the IT guys to help him read the memory card. The ride back to the station was uneventful.

"Good afternoon, Detective," the desk sergeant greeted him.

Adam gave him a nod and a quick greeting before heading to his office. He wanted to check his emails and phone messages first, then see about a reader for that memory card.

Adam stopped in the break room and grabbed a cup of coffee. His night on the couch had not been as restful as he'd let Emma believe. What he couldn't decide was if it was because of the comfort of the furniture or because he was in Emma's home for the first time in so many years. Having her back in his life had begun to fill a void he hadn't realized existed, and it had him a little off-balance.

Settling into his chair, he booted up his computer

and logged into the email program. Mostly there were departmental announcements, wanted posters, and a random weather report from one of the IT guys who probably should have been a meteorologist instead.

After deleting all the junk and saving the important stuff, he ran across one random email from an address he didn't recognize. The subject simply read Important Information. He clicked on the email and opened it.

Stay off the mountain and we will leave your girl alone.
What matters more to you—a big bust or saving her life?
You back off. We back off.
Case closed.

A knot formed in his stomach. They knew who he was. Not good. Not good at all. Adam looked around his office as though the sender of the mysterious email would somehow be standing behind him.

The email was a generic one, giving away nothing about the sender. It didn't matter though; he knew who it came from. Well, not exactly. But he had a good general idea. Fishing his cell phone from his pocket, he dialed Emma's number. It took her three full rings to answer, making his leg bounce up and down in an effort to free the nervous energy beginning to engulf him.

"Hello?"

"Emma! Are you okay?" He really hadn't meant to sound so worried.

"I'm fine. Why?"

He ignored her question. "Can you just double check the doors and windows?"

"Adam? Did something happen?" Now she sounded as worried as he did.

"Nothing. I just want you to be sure they are all locked." He could hear her moving around, probably going from door to window.

"Adam Marshall, you have always been a terrible liar. Tell me what's wrong."

He sighed and leaned back in his chair, still studying the email on his computer screen. "The men that are after you also know who I am."

"How do you know?" There was a slight tremor to her voice. Emma had always been fearless. The first in their group to try skateboarding, rollerblading, and bungee jumping. At that moment though, he heard the hint of fear that having her name on a hit list caused. The fear she'd been working so hard to keep in check.

He might as well tell her. Emma deserved to know. "I got an anonymous email at work. They told me to back off the case and they'd back off you. Told me to choose, your life or the big bust."

Emma exhaled hard against the phone, her breath causing a little static between them. "You can't give up the case."

"I can't risk your life." The conviction in his voice came from the soul.

"You've put in too many hours, Adam. That email just means you're getting close. Someone is really worried."

Adam drummed his fingers on the desk. "There's too much risk. If I hand over the investigation to the rest of the task force, it will keep you safe."

"There's no guarantee of that. I'm a loose end, remember? Whether you keep investigating or not, they are going to keep looking for me."

He leaned back in his chair and crossed one leg over the other. "I'm not sure I'm willing to take that chance."

"So, you'll give up everything you've worked for, put your career and reputation on the line? For what? A hunch."

"I can't lose someone else I care about. This is just a job."

"A job you love. A job you were meant to do since you were a baby!" Her obvious frustration echoed his own.

He slapped a palm onto the surface of his desk, the sting of it traveling all the way up his arm. "It's just a job. You are too important to me to risk losing you all over again."

Emma chuckled. "You make it sound so serious."

He jumped to his feet and paced the area behind his desk. "It is serious!"

A uniformed officer passing by stuck his head into Adam's office. "You okay in there, Detective?"

He waved the officer away. "I'm fine, Collins."

"Adam? Are you still there?" Emma asked.

Adam went and closed the door so no one else would interrupt them. "Yeah, sorry. One of the guys stopped by but he's gone now. Did you make sure everything was locked?"

"Tight as a tuna can."

He couldn't help but laugh. "Tight as a tuna can?"

Emma laughed too. "My great-granny used to say that. Always seemed logical to me. Now, back to the important stuff. What are you bringing me for dinner?"

Resting his feet on his desk, Adam reclined the desk chair and let his eyes close. "You are infuriating sometimes. You know that, right?"

"Only on days that end in Y. Bring me food. Preferably Italian. Then we can talk about what to do with the case."

"There's nothing to discuss. Now that they know who I am too, I should hand it off. I'm sure the FBI, ATF, and state police can handle it without me."

Emma chuckled. "Alphabet soup."

Confused, Adam frowned. "You want me to bring you alphabet soup?"

"No, silly. The FBI and ATF. My boss always called the government agencies alphabet soup."

"Ah, okay. I was about to question your definition of Italian food." He lowered his feet to the floor.

"You can't hand it off. You need to see things through, Adam."

Truth be told, he didn't want to give up. He wanted to protect Emma *and* see the investigation through to the end.

"I'll think about it, Em. There's a lot of things at stake. Right now though, I've got to meet with a buddy in IT about a couple of things and then I'll bring you enough food to feed the local high school football team."

"Gee, I'm not that hungry. Eh, forget it. Yes, I am. Bring it on, buddy."

The stress from the email finally melted away. "You got it, woman. See you in a couple of hours."

They ended the call, and Adam printed a copy of the email to bring with him. He also printed a copy of the one

Emma had sent to him. Maybe his buddy John could figure out more than he had from the email addresses.

Since the police station sat next door to the operations building, the contractors had had the foresight to build a tunnel between the two buildings. On the other side of operations sat the main fire station, also connected by tunnel access. Adam took the stairs to the basement and headed to the passageway. He patted the pocket of his shirt where the small memory card sat. For the first time since Emma had walked into the precinct, he felt hopeful that they might break this case wide open. Obviously, the sender of the email didn't know what he'd found, so maybe, if there was something good stored on it, he could close the case quickly and protect Emma at the same time.

CHAPTER 13

"Hey, John." Adam knocked on the office door of John Burns.

John looked up from the computer he was working on. "Adam! How nice to see you." The older gentleman stood and offered Adam his hand. Adam accepted the handshake.

"I got something I need you to look at. I don't have the little doohickey you need to plug it into my computer." He pulled out the memory card and handed it to John. "And you know how old the department computers are."

"Dinosaurs." The other man nodded as he looked at the card in his palm. "No worries. I got you covered, brother."

He popped it into a slot on his laptop. "This will just take a second to open up. Gotta load the driver first." John clicked an icon then tapped a tune on his desk with his fingers while they waited for it to load. He raised an eyebrow at Adam. "I heard Emma's back in town."

"Yeah."

John raised both eyebrows this time. "I also heard someone's trying to take her out."

Blood rushed through his veins, pounding in his ears. "The whole damn department knows already? Carter and his big mouth."

"What does Carter have to do with this?" With a confused look, John held up his hands in surrender. "Hey, man. I didn't know you asked your boss for permission to date a chick, but if that's what you do, no judgement here. We all knew it would happen eventually."

Adam's burst of anger receded quickly. John meant take Emma out on a date! "Sorry, man. I'm just a private kinda guy, you know? People talking about my personal life gets under my skin."

John shrugged. "Whatever, man. Sorry to get you all worked up. Here's your file." He moved the mouse cursor over a yellow file icon and clicked.

A list of dated files appeared. "Where did you get this? A camera?"

Adam nodded. "Yes. A security camera." Probably more like a spy camera but it didn't matter.

"I'm guessing it was motion activated." He pointed to the computer screen. "See how they are all date and time stamped?"

Adam followed the list down to the date and time that Emma would have witnessed the murder. He pointed to the right one. "Can you click on that one, please?"

John moved the cursor to the indicated file and clicked. A few seconds later, a video loaded. In it were two men, one tied to a chair and the other holding a gun to his head. The way the shooter stood, he looked straight at the camera as though he didn't know it was there.

A perfect face shot. "Can you freeze it there and print me a picture of that man? He's my suspect."

"Sure thing." John clicked a few things, and in a minute the color printer beside them booted up and spat out a photo of the killer.

Adam picked it up. He definitely looked like the guy at the supermarket. "Who are you, you slimy-looking dude?"

John peered at the photo and faked a shiver. "Definitely not someone I'd like to meet in a dark alley."

"Anyway we could download those files to a jump drive? I won't necessarily have secure internet access the next time I open them. "

"Sure thing." John pulled a jump drive out of another drawer, plugged it in, clicked a few things, and popped it out. He handed it to Adam. "Anything else I can help with? I like living vicariously through you, my crime-fighting friend."

Adam laughed. "Actually, there is one more thing. Is there any way to know who sent these emails?" He handed the printouts he'd made to John.

"Not from these pieces of paper. But if you wanted to forward me the original emails, there's some investigating I can do from there."

"Okay. Hold on, I'll do it right now." Adam pulled out his cell phone and signed into his work email. "There. Sent."

A little chime sounded on John's computer. "Got it. I'll look at it as soon as I finish this thing I'm working on for the chief."

"Thanks for all your help. I really appreciate it." They bumped fists, and Adam headed back to his office. He wanted to grab his laptop to take to the cabin. He could watch the videos there. Leaving Emma for too long had started to worry him. And, if he were being completely honest, he missed her.

* * *

Emma walked into the kitchen area and pulled open the refrigerator. Bottles of water lined the top shelf. Soda and beer filled the next one. The bottom shelf held some packages of steak, chicken, and ground beef. She could see that the vegetable and fruit drawers were also full. She would have to ask Adam how it all got there. Keeping fresh food in a fishing cabin seemed odd. But then, the whole place was kind of odd with its modern décor.

Pulling out a bottle of water, she closed the door and started opening cabinets. Dishes, glasses, and serving pieces filled one. Another held rows of canned goods. Emma reached up and pulled one out. Canned beef stew. The last time she'd eaten that, she'd been in college.

Footsteps sounded on the front porch. Emma froze. There was no way Adam had made it back that quickly. Maybe he had sent one of his brothers like he'd mentioned. Quietly setting the can and bottle of water down on the counter, she looked around for something to defend herself with. The footsteps moved closer. Emma spotted a broom hanging on a hook in the corner of the room. Grabbing it, she held it in front of her like a baseball bat. The doorknob jiggled, followed by the sound of a key in the lock.

Okay, maybe it was Adam.

Just in case, Emma walked quietly across the space and stood behind the door. As she readied the broom, the door pushed open. The intruder whistled a tune, low and quiet. Emma raised the broom.

He closed the door, and Emma made her move.

"Freeze!"

The man dropped the cooler and the bag he carried and spun around, hands out at his side. "What? Who?" He wore a navy-blue Boston Red Sox hat, matching T-shirt, and a look of shock. A long gray ponytail ran over his shoulder, and familiar blue eyes peered back at her. Familiar, but not.

"Who are you?"

"I should ask you the same thing." He looked her up and down, a smile twitching the corner of his lips when he noticed her broom. "What are you doing in my cabin?"

"Your cabin?" Now she knew why his eyes were familiar. "Are you Adam's uncle?"

"Walt Marshall. Now that you know who I am, who are you?"

Emma leaned the broom against the counter. "I'm Emma Thomas. A friend of Adam's."

"Emma Thomas, Adam's little friend from grade school? Now you're the big-time newspaper reporter."

She nodded. "You know my work?

"Of course! Why is an investigative reporter snooping around my fishing cabin?"

"I'm not snooping. I'm hiding." She knew that sounded

weird as soon as the words left her mouth. "What I mean is, I'm in hiding. A story I'm working on got tied up with a case Adam is working, and I made some people mad. Adam brought me here this morning. He should be back soon."

Walt grinned. "So, you're in like witness protection?"

"No. Kinda. Not really." Emma laughed. "It's not official or anything, but I am hiding out for protection. Just until we can figure out who wants me dead."

Walt pressed a hand to his heart. "Oh my! You got a hit man after you? This is better than the TV."

Emma laughed. "So glad to entertain you."

"So, my nephew brought you out here to hide you away while he goes after the bad guy?" Walt looked proud.

"I went to Adam when I needed help and ended up here in this very beautiful cabin. I was quite surprised by the inside, by the way. The exterior is deceiving."

Walt shrugged. "I figured if it looked run-down and old, no one would try to steal my television."

"Good plan, Mr. Marshall." Of course, she didn't mention that the other old, run-down cabin she'd encountered that week served as an outpost in an organized crime transport route. It also hosted murders, apparently.

Emma's phone chimed with a text in her pocket. She pulled it out.

Adam: I'm on my way.

She debated telling him that his uncle had shown up unexpectedly and decided to wait. Her stomach let out a loud rumble, making Walt chuckle. It felt like forever since they'd had lunch.

"You know, there's plenty of food in this here cabin. My nephew isn't trying to starve you, is he? You already could stand to eat a couple cheeseburgers."

Her own uncle had said the same thing earlier that day. She wanted to be offended by his comment, but the smile on his face told her he wasn't being nasty. "I actually had a huge burger for lunch at my uncle's diner, and Adam is bringing me dinner from the Italian place in town. I had a craving for carbs. All this running for my life has struck up quite an appetite."

"I like you." Walt winked. "I bet my nephew does too. He needs a feisty one to keep him in line. The good Lord knows you can sure work a broom handle."

Her face warmed as every ounce of blood in her body seemed to go straight to her cheeks. "Yeah, sorry about that. I thought you might be the guy trying to kill me."

Walt nodded toward the broom and grinned. "No one ever told you not to bring a broomstick to a gun fight?"

Emma laughed, dropping her hands on her hips. "Hey, a girl's gotta improvise, you know?"

He leaned over and picked up the cooler he'd dropped earlier. "I'm just gonna drop these cold cuts and salads in the fridge and I'll be on my way. You and that nephew of mine feel free to eat whatever tickles your fancy."

"Adam just sent me a text that he is on his way. Why don't you wait and have dinner with us?" Emma grabbed some wrapped deli packages from the cooler he set on the counter and handed them to Walter, who stashed them in the refrigerator.

"You all don't need some nosy old man hanging round on your dinner date."

Emma laughed. "I'd hardly call it a dinner date."

"Adam's kinda a grab-and-go bachelor. He keeps frozen burritos and microwave meals in his kitchen and not much else. The very fact that he is going to sit down and eat off a plate like a civilized human will have his Aunt Stella tickled pink. And she'll whack me with her broom if I horn in on this meal of yours."

"It's really no bother." Emma put the last salad in the refrigerator and closed the door.

Walt closed his cooler and walked back over to his discarded duffle bag. "The fish are always bitin' out here. I'll be back. Tell my nephew to let me know when he catches the bad guy."

Emma smiled at the older man. "I most definitely will. It's been very nice meeting you, Walt."

He reached up and tipped the cap of his baseball hat. "Likewise."

As Walt put his hand on the doorknob, footsteps sounded on the porch. "It's me, Emma!" Adam called through the door.

Walt pulled it open. "Hello, nephew!"

"Uncle Walt! I'm so sorry. I forgot to tell you I'd be using the cabin. I remembered as soon as I saw your truck." Adam motioned to a blue pickup truck parked beside his marked police vehicle.

"No worries, boy. I was just getting to know your friend. She's a pro with a broomstick, so you better watch out.

She'd make my Stella proud."

Adam walked in while Walt talked and put the big paper bag he carried on the little table in the kitchenette. "Do I even want to know what that means?"

"Probably not. A girl's gotta have a few tricks up her sleeve." Emma winked at Walt. "Right, Walt."

"Please, call me Walt. A young lady like you callin' me Mr. Marshall sends my AARP status through the roof."

"All right, Walt. It's been a pleasure meeting you. Thank you for letting me borrow your little hideaway for a few days." Emma gave him a quick hug. "I'm going to go wash up quick before dinner."

Emma stepped into the little bathroom and closed the door. She could hear the muted voices of Adam and his uncle, so she stayed in there until she heard the front door close. The last few days had been a blur. Maybe she could finally sit, eat, and relax with her old friend—pretend for a little while that everything was absolutely normal and they were just two people sharing a meal.

CHAPTER 14

Patting her hands and face dry on a towel hanging by the sink, Emma left the bathroom. The entire cabin had filled with the aroma of sauce and cheese while she'd been hiding.

"That smells so good." Emma walked over to the kitchenette where Adam had already laid out the spread of food he'd purchased.

"There's ziti, meatballs, chicken parm, fettuccine alfredo, and of course garlic bread." Adam made a sweeping motion in the direction of the food. "You can have whatever you want."

Emma picked up a plate. "I think I'm just going to have some of everything."

Adam pulled out some serving utensils and they filled their plates to capacity. Once they were settled at the tiny table, Emma dug in. "Mmm… this is so good."

"I'm sorry about my uncle showing up like that. I kept meaning to call him and with everything going on, it just slipped my mind."

"It's okay." Emma pointed to the broom still leaning

against the counter in the corner. "I'm a master with a broomstick."

Adam frowned. "What exactly happened with that broom anyway?"

"I don't swat and tell." Emma popped a bite of chicken in her mouth and winked at him.

"How much did you tell Uncle Walt about why you're here?" Adam twirled spaghetti around his fork.

"Just enough to explain why I was creeping around his fishing cabin without his knowledge." Emma got up and went to the fridge. "I need a drink. You want one?"

"Water would be great, please."

She grabbed a couple of cold bottles and put the one she'd opened earlier back inside to get cold again for later. Handing one to Adam, Emma sat back down and cracked hers open.

"Thank you," Adam said, also opening his and taking a long drink. "I told Uncle Walt we'd hopefully only be here a couple of days."

"Really? What makes you think so?"

Adam pulled two folded pieces of paper from the pocket of his flannel shirt and handed them to her. The first was a color photo. She dropped them both when she got a look at who was in the picture.

"That's the murder I witnessed."

Adam nodded. "Yeah."

She picked it up again and studied it. "How did you get that?"

Adam took another bite of food and chewed it slowly

before answering. "I went back to the cabin after I brought you here and took another look around."

She pointed to the photo of the killer. "So, is that how you got this picture?"

"There was a hidden camera in the cabin. A little statue of a grizzly bear. I popped the memory card out, and a buddy in IT pulled the files for me."

This caught her interest. "What else did you see on the camera?"

Adam shook his head. "Nothing yet. I figured I'd watch the videos tonight."

"We can watch them tonight, isn't that what you meant?"

"Emma, this is a police investigation. A joint task force of government agencies is in place to take these guys down as soon as I give the go-ahead. This isn't just about an exciting news story anymore."

"I know. It's just—I need this story. More than you know." She got up and walked to the sink to rinse her plate.

Adam rose from his chair and walked over to where she stood. He lifted her chin with his finger so she had to look at him. "This is so much bigger than that now, Em. This investigation is months in the making. As much as I'd want to do anything I could for you, I can't jeopardize that. You know that."

Adam's touch confused her. Her mind wanted to be angry at him for trying to cut her out of her story but her heart wanted to turn in to his arms and let him hold her until it was all over.

"I understand, Adam. I really do. But you'd never have

known about that cabin unless I told you. I deserve to get the story on this."

Adam's eyes were dark, like a storm brewing over the mountains, as he stared at her. "I will give you everything I can, I promise. As soon as the investigation is over. Right now, though, I have two goals—keep you safe and break up the drug ring. Their use of our town as their transfer station puts a black mark on Staunton I'm not willing to tolerate."

Emma reached up and straightened the collar on the flannel shirt he wore. As a kid, he had always been half a mess. One shirttail untucked, unruly hair, a half-popped collar. Emma liked things neat and orderly and had always been the one to keep him straight. It was kind of nice to do it again. She smiled up at him. "I feel the same way. This is our home, and I hate what these criminals are doing to it."

He toyed with a strand of her hair. "So, you'll behave and let me do my job?"

She pushed him away. "I'm not a child, Adam."

Adam put his arms around her and pulled her close. Emma studied the floorboards, hoping Adam didn't notice the heat in her cheeks. She couldn't be sure it was from her anger at him rather than his nearness. She chose to believe the former.

"Look at me, Emma." He spoke softly, but there was something different in his voice. Something she hadn't heard there before. Not when they were kids, and definitely not in the last few days. "Emma? Please."

Slowly she looked up at him. He had those storm clouds in his eyes again. "What?"

"You are the farthest thing from a child. When I look at you, I see a woman. A woman I want to know better. A woman I never thought would ever walk into my life again. Fate brought you back to me, and I'm not about to take that lightly."

A single tear escaped the corner of her left eye and ran down her cheek. "I don't want to lose you either. You were the best friend I've ever had. We should have supported each other after Miranda's death, not run away from each other. Maybe if we had, so many things would have been different."

***

So many things would have been different.

He watched that tear as it traveled over her smooth skin and dripped from her chin onto the front of her T-shirt. The anguish in Emma's eyes told him there was so much more going on than he could ever guess. He'd suspected her sudden return to Staunton meant more than house and dog sitting for her parents.

"This is not how I wanted to have this conversation but I think we should just do it now. We can't keep dancing around it." Adam took her by the hand and led her to the sofa. He waited while she sat down, then settled in next to her.

Emma moved so that they didn't touch, sending the world's sharpest dagger straight through his heart.

"What do we do now?" She picked at a thread on one of the throw pillows. His whole life, Aunt Stella had always had a thing for pillows. Tonight, Emma clutched one with a rainbow-colored fish embroidered on it to her midsection, letting it distract her gaze from his.

"We talk. About that night. And everything else that has happened since."

She looked up at him then, tears streaming from both eyes. "Aside from you, Miranda was my best friend in the world. Losing her was the hardest thing I've ever had to go through. Second only to losing your friendship at the same time."

Her words widened the crack in his already damaged heart. "I'm so sorry, Emma. I just didn't know what to do. We were kids and I couldn't figure out how to handle the guilt."

She shrugged. "So you cut me out of your life?"

"I thought it was my fault. I knew Miranda liked me. I shouldn't have kissed you when I knew she'd come there expecting me to ask her to dance, to kiss her. I felt like I'd not only taken her life but ruined yours."

"We both were there. You kissed me, but I wanted it as much, if not more, than you."

Confusion filled his head. "You wanted me to kiss you? Even knowing how Miranda felt?"

She tossed one of the throw pillows at him. "Of course, I did. You were my first love, you silly boy."

"Miranda didn't know either, did she?"

Emma shook her head slowly. "I never told anyone until just now. You talked about us being friends so much, I figured I was permanently friend zoned."

Her words swam in circles in his mind. She'd wanted him to kiss her. Her first love. It was all becoming so surreal. "I thought if you knew I wanted to be more than your friend, I'd lose you completely. You never showed interest in anything other than friendship."

"Adam, you were the star athlete. Girls loved you, and you definitely seemed to love their attention. I wore thick glasses and carried a notebook with me everywhere hoping for a big story for the school paper. We really weren't well matched."

Adam shrugged. "That's where you're wrong. We were perfectly matched. Opposites that complemented each other exactly. You kept me balanced. Plus, your glasses were pretty adorable."

Emma felt her cheeks flaming again. "I thought that night, once you kissed me, maybe we had a chance. Then, after Miranda's accident—" She picked at a loose thread on the rainbow fish. "You wouldn't talk to me."

"So that's why you left town the second we graduated?"

"I was so embarrassed. And lonely. I didn't have Miranda, and I didn't have you. I couldn't even go to church. I felt like everyone there blamed me for being a bad friend. I blamed God for letting her die. It was all so overwhelming."

"I could never go back there either, much to my mother's chagrin. She still claims that no one blames me, but I don't believe her. Miranda's parents definitely did."

Emma tossed the pillow aside and looked Adam in the eye. "Miranda made a choice that night too, you know. It's taken a lot of years for me to come to terms with it, but she is the one who chose to speed on that road in bad weather. She knew how icy it got on that curve, yet the police said she never even tried to slow down. There were no skid marks or anything."

Adam sighed. "I know. I read all the police reports too."

"Miranda always thought she was invincible. And she loved drama. Her huge dramatic exit was probably just for attention." Emma wiped the tears from her eyes with the backs of her hands. She picked the pillow up again and hugged it, not saying anything for a long while. Finally, she set the pillow on the coffee table and reached out for his hand, giving it a squeeze. "She also changed her crush more often than I check my phone messages. If she hadn't overreacted like that, she'd have moved on to the next guy by the following week. Maybe even by the next day."

The tears seemed to have washed away most of the pain. Emma's green eyes were bright and clear once more as she looked at him. He wanted nothing more than to pull her to him and kiss away the rest. But he still had something to say. Something he'd held on to for almost his entire lifetime.

He ran his thumb lightly across her palm, liking the way his large hand fit so perfectly with her more slender one. He chuckled. "Friend zone, huh?"

Emma laughed. "Well, yeah."

"I never, ever wanted you in the friend zone. I fell in love with you the first day we met."

She laughed again and tried to pull her hand away, but Adam held tight. "We were in second grade."

"And you were the prettiest second grader I'd ever met

with one heck of a mean right hook. The way you knocked Russel Brooks to the ground when he stole my lunch box—well, you stole my heart." Adam knew his skin had taken on a deep crimson blush but he didn't look away. "Losing you was the hardest thing I've ever dealt with. Worse in some ways than losing my dad or Leslie. The day you left Staunton, you took a huge piece of my heart with you."

Emma reached up and pressed her palm to his cheek. "I missed you so much. Everyone I dated I compared to you and no one ever stacked up. Not even—"

Adam wrapped his fingers around her wrist and pressed a kiss to her knuckles. "Not even who, Emma?"

She looked away. "There's a reason I left Richmond, and it had nothing to do with my parents' trip. That was just a convenient excuse."

"What happened?" Adam asked, concern thick in his voice.

"I made the biggest mistake a reporter can make. It cost me my job and my reputation."

Adam slid from the couch to the floor and knelt in front of her. "Tell me."

Emma shook her head, eyes closed and tears leaking from under her lashes. "I let my heart take over my head. I got involved with my boss. I had no idea he was married or that I was only one in a long line of young reporters he'd preyed on. When I got a big promotion, someone found out about our relationship and spread it all over that I'd slept my way to the top. Basically, I was just a big office joke."

"Oh, Emma. I'm so sorry."

She held up a hand. "Wait. There's more. Human resources found out. There was a policy, and I knew. My heart just didn't care. I got fired. And so, here I am."

"But the big story?" Adam looked confused.

"Freelance. All of this happened well over a year ago. My reputation has been in the toilet. I thought a huge exposé like this would offer me redemption in the reporting world. And now I've gone and messed that up too."

"You haven't messed anything up."

Emma sighed and leaned back into the cushions. "You don't understand how it works."

"One thing I have always held on to that has gotten me through the worst is that everything happens for a reason. I have no idea why a serial killer murdered Leslie or your boss cost you your job, but in the end, all those things brought us to this point." He leaned forward a little bit, grasping both her hands in his and lightly tugging her in. Emma didn't resist, and that made his heart sing. "When you walked into my precinct, a tree branch stuck in your hair and dirt smudged on your nose, I'd never seen anything more beautiful. I've missed you so much, Emma."

"I've missed you too." She leaned in a little more. The light feather of her breath against his skin set his heart beating in double time.

Adam closed the tiny space between them, pressing his lips to hers. Emma slid her hands up over his chest and wrapped them around his neck, pulling him in closer. Adam moaned against her lips, prompting Emma to part them and allow him to deepen the kiss. His blood roared and his heart soared.

He'd waited so long to tell her how he felt, never imagining she felt the same. Nor did he expect to confess his love under these circumstances but if life had taught him anything, it was that tomorrow was never guaranteed.

His phone chose that moment to sound off, bouncing around on the table where he'd left it.

"You better answer that," Emma murmured, sitting back into the corner of the sofa, smiling softly at him.

"Yeah." He knew he should but answering that phone was the absolute last thing he wanted to do.

CHAPTER 15

He picked up the phone and hit the answer button. "Marshall."

"It's Burns. I took a look at that email you forwarded to me."

He'd totally forgotten about that email. Emma watched him quietly, questions in her eyes. He held up a finger, indicating he'd explain in a minute. "Find anything I can use?"

"Unfortunately, probably not. The IP address tracks back to the open computers at the public library. I already called over there and they don't keep any records of who uses which machine when."

Adam got up and paced the small space. This was not the news he wanted. "What about the email account? Could you get anything from that? Even the tiniest detail could help me find this guy."

"Sorry, Marshall. The name, address, and phone number were all fake."

He dropped down on the couch next to Emma again.

"Thanks for checking it out for me."

"Anytime, buddy. Hope you get your guy." John disconnected the call before he could say anything else.

"What did I miss?" Emma asked.

Adam stood and walked over to the table, where he grabbed the printout of the email. He handed it to Emma. "I got this today."

As she read it, the color slowly leached from her face leaving Emma pale as a ghost. "Is it from the same person who sent me the one I got this morning?"

"I'm not sure, but it's likely."

This time Emma got up and paced the small space. "What are you going to do? I know you wanted to hand it over, but you can't let the case go."

As she passed in front of him, Adam caught her wrist. "I'm not going to let them hurt you."

She looked down at him, her green eyes full of conviction. "I know. I'm safe here. As long as I'm with you, I'll be okay. You have to keep working this case."

Adam stood and pulled her into an embrace. "I can still pass it off to someone else. ATF and the FBI are both dying to take the lead."

She pushed back against his chest. "No! You can't. You—we—have to solve this case. Together."

Adam toyed with a stray curl that had escaped her hair clip. "Like I said before, is the story really worth risking your life for?"

"It's not just about the story anymore, Adam. It's about doing what's right. They are using our town, our home to spread their evil. Drugs. Death threats. If we don't take a stand now, who's to say what they will do next. Steal our children? Sell their drugs in our schools? Staunton is a peaceful place but it won't be if someone doesn't put a stop to them. You are that someone. All it takes for evil to prevail is for good men to do nothing."

"Edmund Burke." Adam took her hands in his and lifted one, pressing a light kiss to her knuckles. If he did that a hundred times, he'd never tire of it. "Okay. We'll fight. But you will stay here until it's all over."

A little smile tugged at the corners of her lips. "Fine. I'll stay here. Unless you do something really cool like stake out the cabin." She elbowed him lightly in the ribs. "Don't try to tell me you aren't planning that. You mentioned it at lunch."

"We'll cross that bridge if we come to it."

"Oh, we're coming to it. And I plan to run full speed to the other side, Detective Marshall."

Adam walked over to the front window and looked out at the pond. Emma had always been so stubborn. Fighting her on it would go nowhere. "I'll consider it, okay? I need to run it by my boss—see if I can use you as an eye witness or something."

"Fine." Emma walked over to the little kitchen area. "I'm going to finish cleaning up in here and then take a hot shower. I feel like this day has gone on forever. After last night, I could use about twelve solid hours of sleep."

Adam looked at his watch. Only seven thirty. "I'm going to make a couple of calls and send a few emails before I look at those files. Take your time. Uncle Walt had an amazing shower installed. Just remember we're on a well, so don't take too much time."

"I can't wait." Emma made a breathy little sound that wrapped around his heart and squeezed. Now that they'd had the talk he'd been dreading, Adam felt anxious to wrap the whole case up quickly so he and Emma could have another very important conversation. He'd be risking his heart, rather than his life, but it would be worth it. Having Emma in his life the last couple of days had set so many things right inside his head and his heart that losing her again wasn't an option.

As he left the cabin to get his laptop from his truck, his phone rang. The number on the screen was for John Burns again. He pushed the call button.

"Hey, Burns, what's up?"

"Pablo Vasquez."

Leaning against the truck, he crossed his legs at the ankle. "Who is Pablo Vasquez?"

He heard some tapping and clicking on John's end before his friend answered. "Only the man that sent you the email."

"How?" Adam asked.

John tapped and clicked a few more times. "I just sent you an email with his last known address, phone number, and most recent mug shot."

Adam looked at his phone screen. The little email icon lit up. "Thanks, man. It just showed up. How did you find him? You said the email address was a fake."

"It was. But it kept bugging me, so I followed a trail of

breadcrumbs he probably didn't realize he'd left, and this is what I found."

"Thanks, buddy. I appreciate you going above and beyond." Adam walked around the back of his truck and opened the tailgate. His laptop bag sat next to his go bag. He grabbed both.

"No problem, Marshall. I love a good rabbit hunt." John laughed and disconnected.

Adam took his bags inside the cabin and set them down on the floor inside the door. He tapped the email icon and opened John's message. Clicking the attachment, he watched as it opened.

The screen filled with a familiar face.

Adam walked over to the table and picked up the photo John had printed for him earlier. Just as he thought—they were the same man. He'd have to send a team over to check out the address.

Dialing the number for the front desk on his phone, he waited for the desk sergeant to answer the call.

"Staunton police, non-emergency number," his brother Jacob answered.

"Hey, little brother."

"Adam! I heard you've been busy. Is it true? You've got the love of your life in protective custody? That's one way to make sure she stays this time!" Jacob chuckled.

"This is official police business, Jake."

"Sure it is." Jacob laughed again. "You alone with Emma... totally business."

"Jacob." Sometimes working at the same place as your

siblings could be a real pain.

"Sorry, big brother. What can I do for you?"

"Can you have a car drive by an address and see if it's legit for me?"

"Sure thing. Give me the address."

Adam read him the information John Burns had provided. "I just need to know if it's a real address, and if it is, is anyone there."

"Gotcha," Jacob replied. "I'll let you know."

"Thanks."

They ended the call. Adam turned on his laptop and waited for it to boot up, then pulled out the flash drive John had loaded for him. "You've been a bad boy, Mr. Vazquez. Let's see what else you've been up to."

He clicked on the yellow file icon and waited for it to open. Once it did, he clicked on the top file and waited for it to load. Two men he hadn't seen before appeared on the screen, both carrying boxes. He watched as they set the two boxes down in the center of the room. The clip ended there. The next one showed the same two guys each carrying another box and adding them to the pile. One of the men then walked over to the kitchen area and reached into the cabinet and pulled out a thick package. He looked straight at the camera. It was the man who had been looking for the ring Emma had found.

His phone rang. He answered the call without looking at the screen. "Marshall."

"Hey, it's Jacob. That address you called about? Empty lot. Used to be a fast-food restaurant that burned down a couple of years ago."

Adam leaned back and rubbed his chin. "Okay, thanks for having someone check it out. I thought it might be fake."

"Sure thing. Stay safe, brother. Oh, and Mom wants you to bring Emma by for dinner this week."

Adam groaned. "You already called Mom?"

"The second after I dispatched that address. Didn't matter though, Carter had already told her."

"I just love having the entire family involved in my business."

Jacob chuckled. "It's the price you gotta pay."

"Yeah, I guess." He ended the call and tossed his phone on the table. He had several more videos to watch and really wanted to be done before Emma returned.

There were several more similar videos. Drug and money drops appeared to happen nearly every day, with a continuous supply train coming and going. Near the end of the list, he saw the murder again. The next one showed Emma poking around the cabin's kitchen area. He knew the very last clip would be him, finding the bear. The videos proved he needed to set up that surveillance and quickly.

With a half dozen phone calls, he secured the people, equipment, and permission he needed to set up watch on that cabin, beginning in the morning.

The water turned off in the bathroom. Emma would be done soon. Shutting off the laptop, he returned it to its bag, then walked around the small space, double checking that the windows and doors were locked tight. The window in the bedroom sat up high in the wall. Long and narrow, it would be impossible for anyone to crawl through. The main space, though, had large windows that looked out over the lake. A beautiful view to most, easy access to an assassin on a mission.

* * *

Emma wrapped her hair turban style in a towel and used a second towel to dry her aching body. Adam had been spot-on about the amazing shower system Walt Marshall had installed. She'd hated to get out but heeded the warning about the well. Pulling on some leggings and a long-sleeved T-shirt, she shook her hair free of the towel, using it to lightly rub the ends. Emma grabbed her hairbrush and headed to the main room.

Adam leaned against a massive bookshelf, pushing his body weight against it.

"What are you doing?"

He looked over at her, his face red with exertion. "Moving this in front of the windows for a little extra protection."

Emma narrowed her eyes and pursed her lips. "Um, I thought you were certain we are safe out here."

Adam gave the shelves one more hard shove. The tendons on his forearm popped out with the exertion. "I'm fairly certain we're safe but it never hurts to err on the side of caution."

"True." Emma walked over and stood next to Adam, hands on the large piece of furniture. "I'll help."

He nodded. "On my count. One, two… three!"

Together they shoved the heavy shelves the rest of the

way, so it nearly covered both windows.

Emma bent over, her hands resting on her hips. She took several deep breaths. "Someone's going to have to put that back when this is over, aren't they?"

"Yeah." Adam took several deep breaths. "Maybe I'll let Uncle Walt worry about that though. He's the one that bought furniture made of solid rock or something."

She plopped down on the sofa. "So, what's next? Pushing a tank up a mountain?"

"Not exactly." Adam sat down in the recliner and pulled the handle to put his feet up. "Ah, this is nice. I may just sleep right here. How was your shower?"

Emma stretched out on the sofa. "You were right about that setup. I plan to build a bathroom just like that in my next home. All those different sprays coming at me at once— perfect medicine for sore muscles. I just don't understand why he went to so much detail out here in this place."

"Uncle Walt's a general contractor. You should see his home. Absolutely gorgeous. The master bathroom there makes this one feel like a high school gym locker room."

Emma sat up and looked at Adam. "Seriously?"

Adam laughed. "Yeah. Like I said earlier, he just likes things a certain way."

She picked up the brush and started working it through her wet hair. Adam stood up and walked over to where she sat, settling in beside her.

Emma yawned. And then yawned again. "I can't believe how tired I am."

Adam reached over and took the brush. "Let me. Turn around."

Emma did as she was told, shifting so she sat cross-legged on the couch with her back to Adam. He ran the brush slowly from the crown of her head to the ends of her hair, midback.

Adam ran his fingers through her hair, following the path of the brush. "Just like strands of silk."

Emma giggled. "It's just hair. Some days I love it and some days I hate it."

"I have always loved it." Adam stroked the brush softly through her hair again. "When you sat in front of me in math class in eleventh grade, the sunlight would hit it in such a way it looked like honey."

With each pull of the brush through her hair, Emma's nerve endings sizzled. She'd never had anyone else do the mundane chore, and with Adam it had become anything but mundane. They sat in silence, the tension between them building. Emma found herself leaning into Adam's touch as he ran his fingers through her now untangled hair.

"I've missed you so much," he whispered, leaning in close to her ear and kissing the softness of her earlobe.

Emma sucked in a breath as her heart skipped a beat. If teen Adam had given her butterflies with his smile, adult Adam had stepped up his game tenfold with his lips. She leaned into the contact, turning her head so that their cheeks touched. "I've missed you too."

Shifting on the sofa, Adam pulled her onto his lap. Wrapping his arms around her, he slid one hand up to the base of her neck. Emma shivered as his fingers brushed lightly along her hairline.

"Emma," he murmured against her lips. She nodded slightly, running her fingers through his hair, mimicking his movements. Adam groaned, pulling back a little. "That's probably not a good idea right now."

"So, you can set my entire body on fire with your touch but I can't return the favor? I don't think so." Emma leaned in and pressed a kiss to the side of his neck, running her tongue lightly over his heated skin.

"Oh, you're a tease, then?" Adam moved suddenly, shifting her onto her back on the couch. "Two can play that game." Pulling on the collar of her shirt, Adam bared her shoulder to his kisses.

"That's not nice! I am *not* a tease." Emma's chest rose and fell rapidly with her racing pulse. Pressing her hands to his cheeks, she pulled his lips to hers. Her whole life, Emma had always loved romantic movies and books. She'd longed for that fireworks-in-the-sky moment that she'd always thought to be made up. The instant Adam kissed her, she felt it all. The fireworks, the flying-in-the-sky-and-dancing-through-the-stars moment.

It was over much too quickly. Adam reached up and pushed her hair back from her forehead. "We need to stop."

"No, we don't." She tried to pull him back down, but he resisted.

"I want to find the killer before we go any further with this. When I make love with you, I want it to be something we both want and something that we'll never forget."

He said when. Emma's heart soared. "I want it. I swear I do."

Adam smiled down at her. "So do I. Just not like this."

Emma sat up and moved over, putting a little space between them. "I'm sorry. I got caught up in the moment. I guess it's time for me to call it a night. Thanks for bringing me dinner, Adam."

He was right, they needed to take a step back. Her head knew it, but her body didn't want to listen.

"There's nothing to be sorry about." Adam rose and walked to the kitchen area, putting even more space between them. "I'll be up early. Setting up surveillance at the mountain cabin tomorrow morning. Do you want me to wake you when I am leaving or let you sleep?"

"Neither. I want to go with you. Just tell me what time and I'll be ready."

He frowned and shook his head. "No. You just stay here where I know you'll be safe, and I'll take care of this. You wanted me to stay on the case, so I am, but I need to know you aren't in danger while I do it."

So much for avoiding any more emotional conversations. "I'll be safer if I'm with you."

"Emma." Adam walked toward her.

She held up a hand to stop him. He stayed where he was. "I want to help. I can identify the shooter."

He ran a hand down his face, pausing to rub the light stubble that had begun to fill in on his chin. She could hear the light scratching noise it made against his palm; the only sound in the cabin, aside from the tension pulsing in the air around them.

"Can we talk about this in the morning?"

Emma tossed her hair over her shoulder so the long, silky strands ran down her back. "Same old Adam. Avoiding conflict with diversion."

"Cut me a little slack, Emma. This is my career at stake. Taking you to an active crime scene and letting you hang out on a multiagency operation pushes a lot of boundaries and crosses even more lines."

She frowned. "I just want to help."

"I know you do. But there's policies and procedures I have to follow. Let me think on it for the night."

"Okay. Then I'm going to quit while I am ahead and get some sleep." She yawned. "I'm too tired to argue about it anyway." She walked to the bedroom and opened the door, then turned back to look at him. "Good night, Adam."

CHAPTER 16

"Good night, Emma. Sleep tight and don't let the bedbugs bite." Adam's words followed her into the ridiculously lavish bedroom. The softness to his tone was reminiscent of days gone by. The last time he'd whispered those exact words, they'd spent half the night wandering the quiet streets of Staunton talking about what they wanted to do after graduation. As she'd climbed in through her bedroom window that night, like she had so many times in their friendship, Adam had whispered goodnight and blown her a little kiss.

Emma turned off the lamps and dropped onto the lush bed. Memories mixed with wishes that things had somehow turned out differently. As sleep moved in and pushed the memories and wishes away, dreams took over. Dreams of a long-ago kiss followed by the vision of a man with a gun to his head. As she tossed and turned that gun somehow turned on her. The leering grin of ponytail man taunting her as he aimed the weapon at her forehead and—

Emma screamed. She kicked and punched and

screamed again. Her body felt tight, bound in place. She couldn't lash out or get away from the man, no matter how hard she tried.

A loud crash sounded, followed by Adam's voice wrapping around her. "Emma! Emma!"

"Adam! I'm here! Help me! Please!" She tried to cry out. The words echoed in her head but made no contact with her ears.

Her body shook as the bonds around her tightened. The man with the gun morphed into empty space all around her.

"Emma! Come on, baby! It's me, Adam. Wake up!"

Adam's voice had grown closer. She struggled to find him in the darkness. "Adam?" His name came out in a whisper.

Strong arms wrapped around her. "I'm here. Wake up, Emma. It's just a dream. Come back to me, sweetheart."

Slowly she pulled herself from the dream and opened her eyes to see Adam's worried expression as he leaned over her. Emma reached up and pressed her palms to his cheeks. "Adam. It's you."

"Yes. You're okay now. It was all just a dream."

She sighed and let her hands drop to her sides. "It was awful."

"Do you want to talk about it?" he asked.

"The gunman was there. He tried to kill me. I was tied up and I couldn't get free." She looked down at the blanket and sheet on the bed. They were wrapped around her like a giant burrito.

Adam ran his hand over her damp forehead, pushing her

wild hair back from her face. "You're safe, Emma. I won't let him get to you."

She reached up and wrapped her fingers around his wrist. "Do you remember when we were kids? All those late-night talks and walks we had?"

"I remember." His eyes confirmed it.

"I never felt afraid. I knew, even then, that you'd always be my protector. I think that's why I went to you when all this started. It's not fair, Adam. I'm so sorry I dragged you into my mess."

He smiled down at her. "Hey, it's my mess too, remember? And besides, if it took a deranged assassin to bring my best friend back into my life, then I'd say it was all worth it."

"It hasn't exactly been the reunion I'd imagined all these years but I'm glad it's happened too. Otherwise, we might have been too stubborn to ever get out of our own way."

Adam looked around the room, then back down at her, grinning. "I only see one stubborn person here."

Emma swatted at him lightly. "Oh hush! You know that's a total lie."

"Go ahead and tell yourself what you have to." He leaned down and pressed a light kiss to her forehead. "Do you think you can sleep now?'

Emma nodded. "I'm sorry I woke you."

"I wasn't asleep yet. My brain decided it needed to rehash the entire past twenty-four hours before letting me rest."

She patted the bed. "Will you stay? I don't want to be

alone anymore. Just to sleep. Like we used to."

Adam studied her for a moment then slowly nodded. "Okay. Just until you fall asleep."

* * *

When he'd heard Emma scream, Adam had flown off the couch and crashed into the bedroom so fast, he'd left his gun on the coffee table. If someone had been in there with her, they'd probably both be dead.

She had him so tied up in knots he'd forgotten everything he knew about procedure and process.

He settled back against the pillows and willed his brain to let him sleep. The clock had already struck midnight, and he had a long day ahead of him, starting very early in the morning.

It felt like he'd barely closed his eyes when the alarms went off on his watch and cell phone. Emma didn't stir, so he slipped off the bed. Adam stretched then headed to the bathroom for a quick shower. When he exited the bathroom fifteen minutes later, Emma stood in the kitchen, dressed and making coffee.

"Good morning," she said as he joined her by the small counter. "I'm really sorry about last night. I don't know what came over me."

He pressed a kiss to her forehead. "We all have bad dreams. It's nothing to apologize for."

She handed him a steaming cup of coffee. "I'll feel better once this is all over. That much I know. But I mean it when I say I'm glad you've got my back."

He took a sip. "Mmm… that's good. From here on out, you can always count on me. I promise. I called my lieutenant last night after you went to bed."

"Oh?" She stopped rinsing a dish and turned to look at him.

Adam scowled. "I don't like what he had to say."

Emma raised an eyebrow with interest. "Which means I'm going to like it."

"He said I could take you back to the mountain but only as a confidential informant doing an identification. You have to stay out of sight and as soon as you ID the shooter, we're out of there."

She gave him the sweetest smile. The kind of smile that could bring a man to his knees. "I'm ready to go whenever you are."

"We should stop for some food. Bagels or something. It's going to be a long day."

Emma nodded. "I packed some waters and a few snacks in a little cooler I found in a cabinet."

"Assuming I'd let you go with me." It was a statement, not a question.

She shrugged. "I hoped you'd changed your mind overnight. Just in case, I wanted to be ready. Plus, I might have overheard you on the phone."

He shook his head. "I don't even know what to say to that. You were eavesdropping?"

Emma gave him an innocent look. "You talk loud. With my ear pressed to the door…."

Adam opened the cooler and peeked inside. "It's like you've done this stakeout thing before."

She tossed her ponytail as she walked out of the kitchen.

"I don't like to be hungry. I get angry."

"So many things that haven't changed." He followed her, yanking her ponytail lightly. "I just need to get a few things and then we can head out."

Adam grabbed his cell phone off the charger where he'd plugged it in the night before, as well as his laptop bag and his truck keys. His holster sat on his hip but he kept his gun in his hand. He handed the bag to Emma. "Can you carry this while I clear the yard?"

She nodded, accepting the bag.

"Stay behind me, okay?"

"Okay."

Adam opened the door and looked out in the yard. Seeing nothing, he stepped outside. "Hold up here, I want to check the sides of the cabin and the truck."

Emma gave him a thumbs up and he slipped along the porch, stopping at one end to slowly look around the side. Everything looked clear, so he moved to the other end of the porch and repeated the process. Once he'd convinced himself that it was safe, he moved to the ground and looked in and around the truck.

He waved to Emma. "Everything's good. You can come out now."

She stepped out of the cabin and pulled the door tight behind her, checking the knob to make sure it was locked.

He pulled open the passenger side door and offered Emma a hand to step up into his truck. She tossed the bag lightly into the back seat and accepted his assistance.

Neither of them spoke until they'd left the dirt road and

hit the highway. Adam reached for her hand and gave it a light squeeze. "You okay?"

Emma looked over at him. "I'm fine. Why?"

"There's tension rolling off you in waves."

"It's still new to me having to be escorted around with an armed guard." She laughed. "I guess that's better than being dead though."

"I'd have to agree with you there." They left the highway and entered a smaller, two-lane road that would take them into town. He always preferred to avoid main roads when he could. That need definitely served a purpose now.

Emma pointed to a street sign. "I remember this road. We used to think it was haunted, remember?"

Adam chuckled. "You might have thought that. I never did."

She stuck her tongue out at him, like she would have done when they were sixteen. "Of course. Adam Marshall has never been afraid of anything."

He'd missed her so much more than he realized. Her teasing him, riding around town together like they hadn't had a care in the world. That something he'd felt like he'd been lacking in his life had been Emma.

"There was one thing I feared back then."

"What?" she asked.

He pulled up to a stop light. Across the street sat the local bagel and donut shop. Their destination. Emma watched him intently, waiting for his answer.

"What were you afraid of?" she asked again.

He took a deep breath and exhaled slowly. "I was always

afraid of losing you."

"And then I left town."

Adam frowned. "Not before I made sure to cut you from my life." A car pulled up behind them and honked. Adam accelerated through the intersection and drove into the parking lot of the bagel shop. He parked the truck but neither of them made a move to exit.

Emma reached over and placed a hand on his arm. "We both made some emotional choices, Adam. What matters now is how we move forward. Time heals all wounds; that's what my mom always says."

He looked over at her. The beautiful girl he'd dreamed about so often in his youth had become a stunning woman who, it seemed, still held his heart in her hands. How could life have kept them apart for so long?

It was pride. The thought flashed through his mind so quickly, he wasn't sure he'd actually thought it.

Pride goeth before the fall. That's what his own mother had always said. A quote he'd never quite understood until just that moment.

"Let's get some food and head up to the mountain. The sooner we get that surveillance going, the sooner we can close this case."

"And get on with our lives?" Emma tossed her ponytail over her shoulder, something else she'd always done when they were young. The early morning sunlight glinted off the natural strawberry-gold highlights.

"Yes." He just hoped she didn't mean their separate lives.

CHAPTER 17

The stop at the bagel shop took less than ten minutes. They grabbed a couple bagels each, as well as a half dozen donuts and a couple of coffees.

"I can't wait to dig into those donuts." Emma opened the bag and took a long sniff of the sweetness it held.

"Uh-uh, little girl. You need to eat your good food first before you have dessert." Adam turned the key and brought the truck's engine to life.

"Bagels being said good food?" She pointed at the other bag on the console between them.

"Of course." Adam reached into the bag and grabbed one. "The cream cheese is the protein."

"Oh, right." Emma laughed and grabbed her own bagel with cream cheese from the same bag.

Adam backed out of the spot and pulled onto the road, headed toward the Blue Ridge Parkway. "The rest of the team should be there by now."

"Do you expect there to be a drop today?" Emma licked some cream cheese off her fingers.

Adam pulled onto the parkway. "If they follow the pattern I found on the memory card, then yes. Sometime after lunch."

"So, all of this could be over by tonight?"

He nodded. "Possibly. If we get the guy who's been after you. That could take a day or two."

Emma frowned. "Oh."

The rest area came into view ahead of them. He pulled off the parkway and drove around behind the building, where he parked the SUV. "Can you give me one of those donuts now? I ate my good food first."

She reached in the bag, pulled out a powdered-sugar-covered donut, and handed it to him. "Don't make a mess."

"Yes, ma'am." Adam took a big bite, sending white powder everywhere, making Emma laugh. Adam laughed with her. "I know you gave me this one on purpose."

She handed him a napkin. "It used to be your favorite. I just don't remember you being so messy about it."

He reached in the bag and pulled out a chocolate-covered pastry filled with Boston cream. "This still your favorite?"

"Of course, it is!" She tried to take it from him, but he took a big bite out of it instead. "Ugh! You're an animal."

He handed it to her. "Want the rest?"

Emma swiped the donut from his hand. "Isn't it some kind of felony to eat someone else's donut?"

"I don't remember seeing that one in the code books." He reached for her donut again but Emma ducked out of the way.

"Oh, no you don't, mister." She turned toward the

window with her snack. "This little piece of heaven is mine, so just back off."

Adam finished his coffee while Emma ate her donut. They both went into the restrooms to wash up and take care of business, then began the climb to the hidden cabin on the mountain.

When they reached the clearing, Adam stopped just inside the trees. "This is as good a spot as any. We can see the front porch and the back of the house."

"Where's everyone else?" As soon as she asked the question, Bill Ryan, an FBI agent from the regional field office appeared.

"Hey, Marshall. Glad you could join us for your op." He pointed to Adam's chin before sticking his hand out to shake Adam's. "You got a little something on ya."

"Good to see you, Ryan." Adam swiped at his chin, coming up with a little bit of chocolate frosting. "Oops. Had us a little snack on the way up." He accepted Bill's outstretched hand, then turned to Emma. "This is Emma Thomas, an investigative reporter from Richmond."

Bill's entire demeanor changed. "You brought a reporter to a sting?"

"She's got clearance from my boss to be here."

"Bad idea, man. Bad idea." He turned to Emma. "I heard you got Pablo Vasquez after you?"

"You know him?" Emma asked.

"He's been on our radar for a while. I'm looking forward to locking him up, for sure. This whole dang thing has been a thorn in our sides for much too long. If this pans out, I'm buying you dinner."

Emma toyed with a piece of hair and gave Bill a smile that made Adam want to throat punch the other man. "Sounds fantastic. I'm sure Adam and I would enjoy that."

Adam secretly enjoyed the look of pain that crossed the other man's expression briefly at the mention of a three-person dinner date.

"Here." Agent Ryan handed Adam a radio. "We're on two. You got an earpiece?"

"Yeah." He patted his jeans pocket.

"I'll leave ya to it then. I still think you oughta send the girl back down the mountain." Bill disappeared into the forest, and Adam pulled out his earpiece.

"Your opinion has been noted. She'll be out of here soon enough."

Bill waved something that looked a lot like his middle finger over his shoulder.

"He seems nice." Emma made a face that told him she meant exactly the opposite.

"Yeah. I'm sure he's a great guy." Adam grunted as he looked around and found an old log from a downed tree that would make a perfect seat for them.

"Is the great Adam Marshall jealous of Agent Bill Ryan?" Emma sat on the log and patted the spot next to her. A large daddy longlegs spider stopped strolling across the wood and looked up at her. Emma grabbed a twig and lifted the arachnid, relocating him the brush beside them.

Adam watched as she moved the spider, then took a seat on the old tree trunk. "Why would I be jealous of him?

He's just another government desk jockey looking for his big break."

"Yup. No jealousy there." She poked him lightly in the ribs. He grabbed her hand and kissed the inside of her wrist.

"You don't fight fair."

Adam winked at her. "Never have. You know that. Shh… do you hear that?" Adam put a finger to his lips. "Sounds like an engine."

"Got an SUV coming up the road to the cabin. Black, tinted windows, Tennessee tags," someone said in his ear.

"There's a truck coming up the mountain," he whispered to Emma.

She nodded.

As they waited, the sound of the vehicle drew closer. A full minute later, the SUV came into view. Adam and Emma watched as the driver pulled to a stop and two men got out of the car. They walked to the back of the truck, opened the gate, and grabbed two boxes.

Quiet chatter filled his ear as the other members of the sting passed around information in excited whispers.

"On my count, we go in," he heard Agent Ryan say.

"10-4." Adam thought about arguing he was in charge but decided it wasn't worth it. Getting the bad guys and their drugs had to be done first. They could hash the credit for the operation out later.

"3—2—go!" Ryan whispered into the radio.

"Stay here!" Adam said to Emma as he took off into the clearing, following four other guys as they breached the porch.

"Drop your weapons!" someone yelled.

"FBI! You're under arrest!" Ryan said.

Adam ran into the cabin and over to where one of the suspects was putting up a fight. "Get down on the floor! Stop resisting!" He plowed into the group, knocking the suspect to the floor. The gun he'd been holding slid across the room and went under an old cabinet.

"Ouch! Did you have to hit me so hard?" The suspect lay on the floor whining. "I need a medic! My neck hurts!"

"Stop crying," Agent Ryan said, snapping cuffs on him. To Adam, he said, "Nice take down. Football player?"

"Varsity, all four years. I always knew that move might come in handy on the job." The team rounded up the two suspects and dragged them outside.

Ryan motioned to them. "I'm going to send these two down the mountain with my two guys over there. We got a transport waiting. The pickup man ought to be here soon, if your intel is correct."

"Sounds good. I'm going to go back and wait with Emma. It shouldn't be but an hour before they show up." Adam went back into the cabin first to grab the suspect's gun. After handing it off to an officer with an evidence bag, he walked back toward the woods and stepped through the trees, expecting to see the old tree with Emma perched on it, waiting for him.

What he saw was an empty tree trunk and no sign of Emma.

"Emma?" he called as loudly as he dared. Maybe she'd snuck off to relieve herself. "Where are you? We got the two guys. Now we just have to wait for the next round."

Only silence responded.

"Come on, Emma. This isn't funny." He walked along the edge of the clearing.

"Emma?" he said once more as he circled back to their original waiting place. When he stepped up to the log, he saw the sunlight catch on something shiny.

He reached down and fished the chain and its pendant out of the long growth around the trunk.

Emma's necklace.

He knew it was hers because he'd given it to her. A really long time ago. He also knew that back then she'd never taken it off. If she still had it on all this time….

Taking a look at the chain, he could see that the links had snapped. They were mangled, like someone had yanked the chain, hard, off her.

Adam made a slow circle, examining the woods around him, praying that Emma would step into view. She didn't. He looked down at the necklace with its broken chain. She didn't because she was gone.

Someone had Emma.

Into the radio he said, "Someone snatched Emma. I've got to go after her."

"Who's Emma?" somebody asked.

"Are you sure she didn't just wander off?" Bill Ryan said. "Maybe she just wanted to get closer to see the big takedown. I told you it was a mistake to have her here."

"So, where is she then?" Adam looked around once more. Desperation was beginning to take over. "I don't see her anywhere."

"Do what you gotta do, man. We got your back here."

"Thanks, Ryan."

"Oh, Marshall?"

"Yeah?"

"Never bring a reporter to a sting."

* * *

Emma looked around the empty space. There was something familiar about the old, run-down building. She just couldn't put her finger on it.

She'd spent the last however long since she'd been kidnapped mentally kicking herself for letting it happen.

As her captor forced her down the mountain, Adam's voice had carried through the trees. She wanted to yell out, but her abductor had slapped a piece of silver tape over her mouth before she even saw him. With her hands tied behind her back, all she could do was move in the direction the gun pointed at her back had told her to.

"You and your copper thought you were so sneaky. No one hides from Pablo. I always get my mark." He'd sounded so proud of himself, bragging about his expertise.

Emma couldn't reply, so they'd just walked along in silence until they made it to the base of the mountain. A black sedan sat parked in the trees. Pablo pushed her toward it. Emma stumbled and fell. Why hadn't he just shot her in the woods?

"Get up!" He yanked her arm, forcing her to her feet. His grip on her burned and had probably left bruises.

She stumbled to the car, where Pablo tossed her in the trunk. A sharp whack to her head with the butt of his gun had knocked her out. When she next saw the light of day, she sat in a chair, arms and legs tied to it so she couldn't escape. At least he'd taken the tape off her mouth. Based on that fact alone, she knew she had to be far away from anyone who might have been able to help her.

Emma caught sight of a field mouse chewing on something in the corner. "Why aren't I dead? I should probably be dead." The mouse looked at her and continued to chew thoughtfully but could offer no insight into her situation.

"Because Pablo is good at taking orders." A voice that sounded oddly familiar came from behind her.

"Who's there?" Emma turned as much as her bonds would allow in an effort to see who had spoken.

"It doesn't matter who I am. In a little while, nothing will matter."

She didn't like the sound of that at all. The little mouse ran across the space, disappearing into a hole in the wall near a closed door. Footsteps echoed around the room, the sound bouncing off the stone walls and floor. Her captor came into view. Emma sucked in a breath of air. "No."

He grinned, pure evil. "Not what you expected, huh?"

"You're supposed to be one of the good guys!" Emma pulled against the ropes that bound her, making the man standing in front of her laugh.

"Don't bother to struggle. I did four years in the Navy before joining the Bureau. I know how to tie a knot. If I were in a beauty pageant, tying impossible knots would be my talent." FBI Special Agent Bill Ryan leaned against a stone wall, arms folded over his chest, an annoyed expression on his face.

Emma stopped tugging at her arms and legs long enough to give Agent Ryan a nasty look. "Why?"

He pulled a pocketknife from his jeans pocket and opened it up. "You showed up at the wrong time. If you hadn't witnessed the murder of another agent, you could have had your little story and moved on with your life."

"The man I saw get shot works for the FBI?"

Agent Ryan ran the tip of the blade he held under his nails, one at a time. "Worked, sweetheart. He worked for the FBI. The only thing he does now is provide worm food."

"Doesn't he have a family? People that miss him and are looking for him? You'll never get away with it."

"I didn't do anything. Pablo did. My hands are clean." He held his hands out, palms up. "See? No bloodstains."

"But you were just there! I saw you at the cabin, arresting those two men. Why would you work so hard to take down your own supply chain?"

He shrugged. "Survival. There will always be more, sweetheart. The war on drugs will never end, because no one really wants it to. Too much money to be made."

Emma stared at the man in front of her, trying to understand, but she couldn't. "But it's your job to enforce laws, not break them. How long have you been on the take like this?"

"What does it matter?" He kicked at a loose stone on

the floor. "The money is good. I have a family to take care of, you know."

"Have you ever heard of working overtime?"

"I work smarter, not harder. And thanks to your boyfriend's boss letting me know he was bringing you along, even catching you was easier. You gave my boy the slip one too many times this week."

"Why didn't he just kill me on the mountain?" Emma asked. "Wouldn't that have been so much easier than all of this?"

Bill sneered. "But not nearly as much fun." He walked over to where she sat and toyed with a piece of her hair.

"Kidnapping is fun for you?"

Bill laughed, the evil sound bouncing off the stone walls and giving her a chill. "Watching Adam Marshall lose someone else he cares about is a ton of fun."

"What did he ever do to you?" Emma demanded.

"The Blue Ridge Killer was *my* case. And he got the arrest. I was supposed to be the one that took him down."

Emma shook her head in disbelief. "You can't be serious?"

"What? You think your man is the only one that can solve a high-profile case? It was supposed to be FBI jurisdiction."

"So, you've got a bruised ego? You held on to that for how many years?"

Bill shrugged. "You made it too easy to get back at him for stealing my fame. I could be a big time consultant by now, writing books on profiling and speaking around the country. There wouldn't have been any need to get mixed up in the other stuff."

A door opened somewhere, bringing with it the sound of running water. Like a river. Suddenly she knew where they had her—the old mill. Abandoned and just far enough out of town to be forgotten; no one would ever find her there. It was up to her to save herself.

Emma had an idea. "So let me help you get out of this so you can claim all the glory on the drug house."

Agent Ryan squatted down in front of her so that they were eye to eye. "There is no getting out of this, little girl."

Emma shrugged, trying to act nonchalant and unconcerned about a criminal being only a few inches from her face. "Depends on how you play it, I guess."

"Hey, boss." Pablo Vasquez walked into the space and scowled at Emma. "You want me to take care of her now?"

Ryan stood up. "Not yet."

"Why not? I been chasing her for two days now. Let me do my job." Pablo paced the small space, waving his gun around. Emma ducked when he aimed it in her direction.

"You aren't going to get to kill her. I am. When I am good and ready." Agent Ryan grabbed for the gun, but Pablo moved faster. He pinned Ryan to the stone wall, his forearm pressed to the agent's throat.

"Let me go, you idiot!" He grabbed for Pablo's arm, trying to free himself. Emma used the distraction to try to free her hands. The more she struggled, though, the tighter the ropes seemed to get.

"I'll let you go if you let me whack her." Pablo pointed in her direction with his gun once more.

"No!" she yelled, jerking to the left and dumping the chair she was tied to on the floor. Her head smacked the cold stones hard. Emma lay there, dazed.

"Relax, little girl. I'm not gonna shoot you yet. I want to enjoy it one hundred percent." Agent Ryan brought his knee up and hit Pablo in the testicles. The gunman doubled over, dropping the FBI agent to the floor. They both lay there, panting.

"Why'd you go and do that?" Pablo whined.

The agent pulled himself to his feet. "You wouldn't let me go. What did you expect me to do?"

Pablo just groaned in response as he also stood up.

"Give me your cell phone." Ryan motioned toward Pablo's pocket.

"Why?" Pablo eyed the phone in Agent Ryan's hand as he pulled his phone out of his pocket. "You got yours right there."

"I got an idea how to end this and get us both what we want." He snatched the other man's phone. "Sit her up again."

"Don't touch me!" Emma tried to kick at Vasquez, but he side-stepped her tied-together legs. Her head throbbed and her vision blurred, but she ignored it. A warm trickle of liquid ran into her left ear.

"Stand that chair up." Agent Ryan held the phone out in front of him. "I need a picture of her."

Emma tried to squirm away, but the chair made it impossible to move. Pablo grabbed the back of the chair and yanked up, dragging Emma with it. Her head flung backward, amping up the throbbing pain. Ryan snapped a photo on Pablo's phone, then pulled his own phone out and looked something up. A few seconds later, he tapped on the first phone, then put it in his pocket. "Now, we wait."

"Hey! Give me my phone!" Pablo reached for the other man, but Agent Ryan sidestepped him.

"I'm not done with it yet."

"Fine. Keep the phone." Pablo pulled his gun again and pressed it to her temple. "Can I kill her now?"

Emma froze, terrified that any movement would make him pull the trigger. She barely took a breath as the two men engaged in a standoff.

"Take a walk, Vasquez. Miss Thomas and I need to have another conversation." Agent Ryan pulled out a gun of his own and aimed it at the other man. "Beat feet."

"Sure thing, Agent. You're the boss." He held his hands up in mock surrender. "But I'll be right outside. No funny business."

"You trying to be *my* boss now?" Ryan asked, but the only reply he got was a slamming door.

He walked over to where Emma sat. Gripping her chin, he forced her to look up at him. His sneer held so much evil in it, a shiver ran down her spine. She tried to pull away but he held tight, squeezing so hard there would surely be bruises. "You should have just stayed in Richmond and left this investigation alone. Of course, after what happened at the paper, I guess you didn't have much choice but to skip town."

"How did you know about that?" Emma's head spun as

she tried to ignore the pain in her jaw.

"I know everything about you, Emma. You're the only child of a retired cop and his nurse wife. You love tulips, eighties' rock, and pizza." He lifted a strand of her hair and toyed with it. She tried not to vomit at his touch. "I also know you left town shortly after your best friend died and haven't been back since—until now. Because you have unfinished business with Detective Marshall."

"Have you been stalking me?"

Agent Ryan let her go, leaned against the wall, and looked at her. "Just doing my homework. Like any good investigator."

Emma shook her head slowly, wincing with the ache in her head and jaw. "I don't understand any of this. Why would you make things worse for yourself by kidnapping me? I didn't know you were involved. I'm one hundred percent sure Adam doesn't either."

He shrugged. "Adam's been working on cracking this case for months. He had no idea where the drop spot was until you came along. A couple more days at the most and he'd have figured it out."

"So, your answer to that was to kidnap me and—?"

Agent Ryan laughed. "Lure him here, of course. I want him to see me kill you. For an investigative reporter, you aren't too quick."

"He won't let you get away with it. You know that, right?" Emma's heart started to ache as much as her head.

"It won't matter. I'm going to make it look like a murder and suicide. The good detective finds you dead and can't live with the guilt of another woman in his life dying because of him."

"And you get to go on being FBI Agent Bill Ryan?"

"Of course." He chuckled. "I'll be the one to discover the bodies."

The phone in his pocket dinged. Agent Ryan fished it out to look at the screen. "Hook, line, and sinker."

"Excuse me? What does fishing have to do with any of this?"

The FBI agent held out the phone, a picture of her on the screen. "Detective Marshall took the bait."

CHAPTER 18

As Adam tore through the forest searching for Emma, his phone vibrated in his back jeans pocket. Pulling it out, he opened the message from the unknown number, praying it was Emma. Maybe she'd borrowed a stranger's phone to let him know she was okay.

What he saw when he opened the message; a picture of Emma tied to a chair. Blood ran down one side of her face, and it looked like she had a bruise forming on her chin. Stone walls and a stone floor surrounded her. Adam knew that place. Too well. He'd partied in that room at the old abandoned mill more than a few times during his high school days . The worn-out structure sat down the end of County Route 3, without another building around for miles. Emma could scream herself hoarse and no one would ever hear her.

He keyed his radio. "Hey, Ryan. This is Marshall. I'm headed to the old mill. He's holding Emma there."

Ryan never replied but another agent did, so Adam moved down the mountain as fast as he could. When he reached his SUV, he hit the lights and sirens and tore out of the lot. All he could think about was Emma. Not calling for backup. Not wondering why Bill Ryan never answered his radio call. Just getting to Emma.

Running lights and sirens all the way up the Blue Ridge Parkway, he didn't encounter much traffic. When he pulled off the exit closest to the mill, he had to slam on his brakes. Traffic sat completely stopped with absolutely no room for him to get around it.

He slapped his palms against the steering wheel. "What is the holdup?" he yelled at all the stopped cars. The light at the intersection ahead was green. He could see no traffic on the other side of the intersection.

Flashing blue lights passed through the intersection slowly, followed by a long black hearse and several stretch limousines. A group of motorcycle-riding police officers passed through next, one of them holding an American flag and another carrying a thin blue line flag. Adam turned off his own lights and sirens as the funeral processional passed, holding his hand up in salute as the procession moved along.

As soon as the last car moved through the intersection and the light turned green once more, the cars ahead of him started driving again. Adam hit the lights and wove his way through traffic until he made it to the two-lane Route 3 heading out of town.

He raced down the pothole-riddled road. As he took a sharp curve, the back tires lost traction and the vehicle slid sideways a good five feet. Taking his foot off the gas pedal, Adam spun the wheel and eventually set the SUV in the right direction. An old, tilted sign on the side of the road said Domici's Mill 4 miles.

Adam switched off the lights and siren and slowed his pace to a near crawl. He itched to slam the gas pedal to the floor, but he didn't. It was better to find a spot to pull over and walk in once he got close enough.

His phone rang. Adam pulled it from his pocket and hit the speaker button. "Marshall here."

"Hey, Detective. This is Dana Murray with the crime lab."

Maybe he should have just let the call go to voicemail. "I'm in kind of a hurry. Can I call you back?"

"This will just take a second. I know you're working a sting, but I think it's relative to what you're doing."

"Fine. Hit me with it." Adam was only about a mile out from the mill, so he started watching for a good place to pull over and hike in.

"The ring you put into evidence? It had a couple different fingerprints on it. They were both in the system. The first came from an unknown source."

Adam nodded even though Dana couldn't see it. "Okay. So, the ring's a bust."

"I'm not sure. Maybe. The other print? This is the one that might be useful. It came from a man named William Ryan. He's with—"

"The FBI."

"Yes, how did you know?" Dana asked.

"He's running point for his agency on this investigation." A little clearing appeared on the left side. It looked like a narrow dirt path leading into the woods. Adam crossed the road and pulled in.

"Hmm, okay. Well, I just wanted to give you the heads-up in case it helped with the sting."

He parked the SUV out of sight of the road. "Wait, Dana. Before you hang up."

"Yes, Detective?"

"How do you think the fingerprint of an FBI agent got on the ring of a criminal involved in a drug trafficking case?" Adam turned off the truck and got out. Locking the doors, he tucked his keys in his pocket and began pushing through the brush.

"He could have shook hands with the man wearing the ring."

"Right. I didn't think of that. Thanks for your input. I gotta run."

"Good luck, Detective Marshall."

He ended the call and tucked the phone in his jeans pocket. A brisk wind kicked up, rustling the trees and sending a mess of dead leaves raining down on him.

His phone rang again. This time he checked the number but didn't recognize it. "Hello?"

"Detective Marshall?"

"Yes."

"This is Special Agent Dyer. Is Agent Ryan with you?"

Adam stopped walking. "No. Why?"

"We can't seem to find him, and he isn't answering his phone. I just wanted to be sure he wasn't with you before we call him in as missing."

First his fingerprint on the ring and now Ryan had gone missing? "Now that you mention it, he never responded when I said I was leaving the stakeout to go to a secondary location. About thirty minutes ago."

"Thanks, Detective. We'll keep looking." Agent Dyer disconnected the call.

The sound of moving water grew louder as he walked. Things weren't stacking up. Agent Ryan's print on the ring. The phone call from Agent Dyer.

The old stone mill came into view. Adam ducked behind a large oak and took a moment to take in the property.

Two cars sat on the bank of the river. A dark sedan with darkly tinted windows and a government-issued sedan. Bill Ryan's car.

Pulling his phone out of his pocket once more, he dialed the precinct and requested a couple of units for backup. Chances were the sedan belonged to Pablo Vasquez. Between the two men, Adam would be grossly outgunned. He snapped a few pictures of each car, including the tags and making sure to get the old mill structure in the background.

Circling around the building, careful to stay in the trees, Adam scouted the layout of the mill. It had been a decade or more since he'd been there; he needed a refresher before devising a plan to rescue Emma. The stones that composed the walls were covered in green and yellow moss. Windows with broken panes circled the structure, too high up for him to see in. Part of the roof had caved in, and the old water wheel sat frozen in time as the river waters ran past it. As he made his way to the front of the building, he heard voices.

Moving carefully, he worked himself into position to see who was talking. One man had his back to him, but he'd recognize that ponytail anywhere. Pablo Vasquez.

In front of Pablo, his face screwed up in an annoyed sneer, stood FBI Special Agent Bill Ryan.

He strained to hear what they were saying. Bits and pieces of their conversation floated in on the breeze over the sound of the river.

"Can I just kill her now?" Vasquez asked, twirling his gun on his finger.

Adam sucked in a breath. Thank God, Emma was still alive. For the moment, anyway.

"Will you stop that, man?" Ryan reached for the gun, but Pablo snatched it back. "You got no respect for the cold steel."

"If you'd just let me do my job, I'd be outta here."

The wind picked up then, the rattle of the bare branches drowning out the next little bit of their conversation. He had to get closer.

Backtracking to the far side of the building, Adam moved as quietly as possible. The old water wheel sat idle, creaky and rotted. Adam crouched low and ran across the small open area and pressed himself up against the stone wall, using the wheel as a little bit of cover. A dirty window was about ten feet to his right, next to the water wheel but up too high for him to see in. Emma could be in there. He had to see inside that window.

A quick assessment of the wood structure seemed like it was sturdy enough to hold his weight if he moved carefully.

The first piece of wood he put his foot on snapped in half. The echo sounded like a gunshot. Adam froze, expecting the two men to come running around the building. When no one showed up shooting, he tried again. This time he tested each board before he grabbed it or stepped on it.

Once he reached the height of the window, he leaned out and peered inside. Emma sat in the center of the room, bound to a chair. Her head drooped forward so that her chin rested against her chest. Her white sweater had crimson stains on one shoulder. A small pool of red liquid sat on the floor a few inches away from the chair.

Using one finger, he tapped lightly on the glass. "Emma!" he whisper-shouted through a hole in the glass probably formed by a rock. "Emma! It's me! Look up!"

Emma showed no signs of life. She didn't even twitch in response to his calls. Was he too late?

Sunlight flooded the dirty room that held Emma. As he watched, Vasquez and Ryan entered.

"What's taking so long?" Vasquez asked Ryan.

"He'll be here. Trust me." Agent Ryan kicked the leg of Emma's chair, jarring her so that her head fell backward. "He's a real cowboy, and he loves her. He's gonna want the whole hero rescue thing to happen."

Pablo paced the room, his agitation obviously growing. "Why does she have to be alive for him to rescue her?"

"You been testing the product or what, Vasquez?"

"What's that supposed to mean?" He shoved Ryan, knocking him to the floor. "You know what? I'm sick of you and your attitude. I got a birthday party to attend tonight for my *abuela*." He grabbed Emma's hair and yanked hard.

"Ouch!" Emma yelled as he yanked again. "Let go of me!"

Agent Ryan stood up, brushing his suit clean. "Step away from the hostage. I promise you'll get your moment soon."

Pablo shoved the gun against her temple. "I'm done waiting."

"No!" Adam shouted through the window. "Leave her alone!"

"I told you he'd show up. Now you get to shoot two—"

Before Ryan could finish his sentence, Pablo took aim at the window and fired two shots at Adam. He jumped back, the wood plank under his feet giving away. Adam fell to the ground, landing hard and knocking the air from his lungs. Scrambling to his feet, Adam ran around the building, slamming the door open and plowing into the mill, gun drawn. Agent Ryan had also drawn his gun and had it pointed at Vasquez.

"Police! Drop your weapons!"

"Detective Marshall! I found Pablo Vasquez." He motioned with his gun. "You want the honor of hooking him up?"

"Put your gun down on the ground, Ryan." Adam moved in closer to Emma.

"You're confused, Marshall. I'm not the murderer in the room!" He waved his gun toward Pablo. "He is. Cuff him, will ya?"

"You okay?" Adam asked Emma.

She nodded toward Agent Ryan. "I'm good. But that

man is not a good man."

"I know." He walked forward, his gun still aimed at Ryan. "Put your hands behind you, Vasquez."

"Yeah, I don't think so." Vazquez rushed Adam, tackling him to the ground and knocking the air out of his re-inflated lungs for the second time.

A fist slammed into Adam's kidney, sending hot sparks of pain through his torso. "Son of a bitch!"

Adam jabbed his elbow into Vazquez's rib cage. With a growl of pain, the other man attempted to wrap an arm around Adam's neck but Adam got his hands up in time to deflect the hold.

"I'm getting so tired of you!" Adam rolled Pablo over, delivering a blow to his chin. Pablo's gun went off, the bullet slamming into Agent Ryan's upper arm.

"You shot me!" Ryan yelled over and over, as he ran over and kicked the other man in the ribs. "I can't believe you actually shot me!"

"Quit your whining." Adam pushed Pablo on to his stomach and yanked at his arms with a loud grunt.

Adam pulled some handcuffs out of his pocket and cuffed Pablo. "Now, stay there, you piece of garbage."

"Take your own advice." Adam looked up to see Bill aiming his gun at Emma. "Stay where you are or I'm going to shoot her right now."

"You don't have to do that." Adam slowly rose to his, holding his own gun on Agent Ryan.

Agent Ryan laughed. "Of course, I do."

"You're hurt. Let me call you a medic before you

bleed out." Adam took a step forward.

"Stay back!"

"Come on, Ryan. You haven't killed anyone yet. Put the gun down and let me get you a medic."

"He's all talk." Vasquez called from his spot on the ground. "That's why he hired me. I get things done. He's just a loud mouth."

Ryan spun around, staggering, his gun on Pablo. "You shut up!"

Adam took a couple steps forward. "You've lost a lot of blood, Bill. You need to get to a hospital."

Bill glared at him, waving his gun between Adam and Vasquez. "It's just a flesh wound." He lost his footing and stumbled. Vasquez took the opportunity to kick him on the back of the knee, sending Agent Ryan flying across the stones. His gun slid across the stone floor as Bill whacked his head on the ground.

Adam sprang at him but the man was out cold. He grabbed the gun from the floor and tucked it into his waistband before hauling Pablo to his feet.

"I need to find something to cut you free with." He shoved Vasquez forward. "Move, Pablo."

"Whatcha gonna do? Take me with you?"

"Nope." Adam dragged the other man over to a storage closet they used to use to play Spin the Bottle and shoved him inside, dropping the wood bar used to lock it into the brackets.

"Hey, man! You can't leave me in here! I'm afraid of the dark!" Pablo banged against the door but it didn't budge.

"There's spiders in here!"

"You're a grown man. You'll be fine!" Adam called back through the door.

"Adam!" Emma screamed. "He's getting away!"

He spun around to see Bill half stumbling and half running from the old mill.

"I'll be back! I promise!" He leaned down and pressed a kiss to her lips. "Don't go anywhere."

"You know I won't." Emma's laugh was the last thing he heard as he ran out the door and the sounds of sirens surrounded him. Three patrol cars whipped into the little lot, cops jumping out. Ryan's car was surrounded by emergency vehicles but he was nowhere to be seen.

"Spread out! Search the woods! The suspect is armed and dangerous, but he is also injured."

"Who we lookin' for, boss?" one of the uniformed officers asked.

"FBI Special Agent Bill Ryan. About six foot, brown hair, wearing an agency windbreaker." Adam ran toward the wood line. "Now, move!"

"I'll take the riverbank!" one officer yelled as he jogged toward the water.

"Are we really looking for an FBI agent?" Adam heard an officer say to another. "Making us all look bad. I hope he goes away for life."

"Yeah, man. Me too," the other officer replied.

"You!" Adam pointed at one of the officers. "There's a hostage inside and perp locked in a closet. Get in there and keep an eye on them. If Ryan returns, shoot him if you have to."

"Gotcha!" he took off at a jog into the mill.

An area of trampled grass caught his attention near the trees. Adam ran to it and dove into the woods, following the trail. Voices echoed through the forest as officers searched for the rogue agent. Adam moved as quickly and quietly as he could. Ryan had a bit of a lead on them, but that man wasn't leaving the area without handcuffs on if he had anything at all to say about it.

Ten minutes later, still following the trail, he stepped back into the clearing behind the old mill.

"You sneaky dog." Adam jogged to the front of the building, expecting Ryan's car to be gone this time, but it still sat in the same spot. "Come out, come out, wherever you are." Adam moved around the building.

"Because you asked so nicely." As Adam rounded the corner to the front of the mill, he found Bill Ryan standing there, gun in one hand and Emma's wrists in the other. Blood trailed in a slow stream down his arm. The bullet hole looked pretty close to his brachial artery. Bill stumbled a little as he pushed Emma in front of him.

"What did you do?" Adam demanded.

"Don't worry, your officer will be fine. He never even knew what hit him."

"He hit him on the back of the head with a sharp rock, took his gun, and shot him," Emma said.

Bill had to be running on pure adrenaline at this point. He'd lost enough blood, he shouldn't have been able to stand upright anymore, let alone take out a grown man with a rock unless he was jacked up on adrenaline.

"Let her go. This is between you and me," Adam said, his gun pointed at Agent Ryan's chest.

"No, I don't think so. She's as much a part of this as you are. If she hadn't seen my man Vasquez shoot that other agent, none of this would have happened."

"You had a fellow FBI agent assassinated. For what? Cocaine or heroin?" Adam inched closer, never lowering his weapon, his eyes on the other man's gun as he moved.

"Nah, man. You know it was always about the money. Have you looked at the retirement plan cops get? I needed to secure my future." Ryan took a step back, dragging Emma with him. His injured arm was his gun arm. Adam could see his weapon visibly shaking as the muscles weakened.

"With drug trafficking? Aren't you supposed to arrest people for that?" Adam closed the distance between them just a little bit more.

"Don't get too close, Adam." Emma sounded scared. "We don't both have to die today."

"No one's dying today, Emma." He purposely spoke to her instead of Agent Ryan, knowing the other man would react angrily. The more energy he expelled, the quicker he'd go down.

"You're not the man in charge here today, Marshall. I know you like to think you got all the answers, but you don't."

Adam motioned around them. "The woods are crawling with cops, man. You don't think you're actually getting away with any of this, do you?" The man was more unstable than he'd thought.

"Once I shoot your girlfriend here and then shoot you, who's going to stop me? I'll be long gone before any of those guys find their way out of the trees. I get to watch you watch her die. Once you're both dead, I'll be the one to find you and take in Pablo. I might even get a medal since Vasquez shot me. I'll finally get the big bust you stole from me when the Blue Ridge Killer was here."

"That's what this is all about? I didn't even care about making that arrest."

"Yeah, well, I did. Now I get my chance for a little fame." He shoved Emma to the ground. "On your knees! Now!"

Emma stumbled and fell into the dirt. Adam caught a glimpse of the determination in her eyes. She had a plan. Something that might actually get her killed, if Adam knew Emma at all.

"Now, Detective Adam Marshall, if you don't want to be responsible for a third death in your pathetic life, drop your weapon on the ground and kick it toward me."

CHAPTER 19

Emma saw the flash of anguish in Adam's eyes when Agent Ryan referenced Miranda's and Leslie's deaths.

"Don't listen to him, Adam. You had nothing to do with Leslie's death. It's not your fault. None of it is your fault."

Adam looked from Emma to Agent Ryan and back again. "I'm sorry I couldn't keep you safe. I tried. I promised you I'd protect you and I failed."

"Waa, waa… we all feel so sad for you, Marshall. Now, you gonna give me that gun or what?"

Ryan shoved his gun into the side of Emma's head. He hit her where the wound was from smacking the floor. The pain shot straight through her and she groaned.

"The only one responsible for any of this is you." Adam stepped forward, his gun trained on Bill. "Don't make me shoot you. I don't want to do that to your family."

"Shut up. Leave my family out of this. " Ryan smacked her in the head again, this time with the grip of his gun. The blow shot sparks of pain through her brain, making the world wobble around her. She squeezed her eyes shut, willing the need to vomit away.

Praying to God that Adam would follow her lead, she threw her body forward. Her face planted straight in the dirt but that didn't stop her from rolling to the side and kicking Agent Ryan square in the groin. He doubled over, the gun he'd held flying from his hand.

Adam was on him in a millisecond, pushing him to the ground and sitting on his back, gun pointed at Ryan. "Don't move. Don't give me a reason to have to go to the department shrink."

Two cops came out of the woods at that moment. Emma called to them at the same time one of them started to speak. "There's no sign of—" When they saw Adam sitting on the FBI agent they'd been hunting, they both ran over.

"Holy cow! Are you okay, miss?" One of the officers helped her to her feet.

"Where did you even come from?" A second officer asked as she untied Emma's wrists.

Emma waved away the concern. "I'm fine. My head just hurts some. I was being held hostage in the mill."

"What happened, Detective?" the first officer asked, pointing at the man Adam sat on.

"Call for a couple of ambulances. He took a bullet, and she's got a head wound." Adam motioned to Emma, then back to Agent Ryan. "Get out your handcuffs. Mine are on the guy locked up inside."

"There's another guy?" The officer helping Emma sounded confused.

"Yeah," she said. "The one who kidnapped me and

tried to kill me a couple times this week because I saw him assassinate another FBI agent. There's also an injured officer in there."

The cop handcuffing Agent Ryan shook his head. "I'm so confused. Why are we arresting an FBI agent again?"

"He's dirty. Been running drug money for months. Put a hit out on another agent and kidnapped Emma. We just put an end to his little operation right now." Adam pointed to the mill.

Adam stood up and pulled Ryan to his feet. "Go put him in your car and radio in for those medics, please. I don't want him to bleed out before he goes to court."

Emma watched as Adam issued instructions, waiting for him to remember her. His gaze finally locked on hers as he walked toward her and pulled her into his arms. She turned her head so she could lean the uninjured side against his chest.

He held her tight, his arms around her making her feel safe and protected. "I'm so sorry."

She pushed back and looked up at him. "Sorry? For what?"

"For letting that monster get ahold of you. I told you I'd protect you, and I let you down."

Emma reached up and held his face between her palms so she could make him look at her. "I said it before, and I'll say it again. None of this is your fault."

He pulled her close again. "I knew something was off about Ryan but I didn't listen to my instincts. If Dana from the lab hadn't called about the cuff link, I might still be trying to figure it out."

"What about the cuff link?" Emma asked.

"It had Ryan's print on it. Pablo Vasquez's too."

An officer emerged from the mill with Pablo in tow. "This your assassin? Found him crying in the corner of that closet. Think he might have wet his pants too."

"Not so tough now, are you?" Emma said as they passed by.

Pablo sneered at her but didn't say anything. The big wet spot on the front of his trousers said enough.

"I want to make a deal. Call my lawyer," Pablo demanded as the cops put him in a cruiser.

An ambulance pulled into the little field, working its way between all the police cars, and stopped near the building. A medic jumped out and went straight to Emma. "That's a nasty bleeder you got there. What happened?"

Emma looked up at Adam and saw his worry. "I hit my head. I'm sure it looks worse than it is."

"Well, we'll get you fixed up in a jiffy," the older man said as he led her over to the back of the ambulance. "Don't worry, sir. I'll take good care of your girl."

The driver stepped down from the ambulance. "I thought we had two victims."

Adam pointed to one of the police cars. "He's in there. Gunshot wound to the upper arm. Don't be gentle."

"Adam! That's not very nice of you." Emma waved him over.

"I'm thinking God might give me a pass on that one." He picked up her hand, wrapping his fingers around hers.

"I'm so glad I found you in time."

"Me too."

The medic dabbed at her head with a saline-soaked gauze pad. "I think this wound's gonna need some stitches. Hop on up into my limousine, my lady, and I will see that the ER docs fix you right up."

"I can drive her myself." Adam stepped between her and the medic.

"Sorry, Detective, but it's policy. I've got to transport her in Big Red here." He tapped the side of the ambulance. "You can meet us there though."

Emma picked up Adam's other hand so she held both of his in hers. "It's okay. Go wrap things up here, and I'll wait for you at the hospital. I'm sure I'll be there a while."

She could see the reluctance in his eyes but he nodded, slowly. "Fine. I did want to be there when they tossed those fools into lockup."

"Go. Do your cop thing and pick me up later. Just know I'm starving. You're gonna have to feed me Mexican or something. Lots of it. Getting kidnapped and held at gunpoint makes me hungry." She leaned up and pressed a little kiss to the side of his chin. "I'm fine, Adam. Really."

"Okay." He looked at the medic. "Remember, you promised to take good care of her."

"Will do." He flashed Adam a mock salute.

They both watched as Adam walked away. "He's in love with you," the medic said.

"We're a long way from love."

"Nope. I've seen love a time or two in my day, and he's

long gone on the love train, darlin'. Now why don't we get you to the hospital and get you fixed up so your man can take you out for that Mexican meal."

He helped Emma into the back of the ambulance and got her settled. The other medic returned and climbed in behind the wheel. "You two all set to roll out?" he asked through the partition.

"Sure thing, Mack. What'd the other guy look like?"

"Oh man, Gary. Got a graze wound. He's lucky. A fraction of an inch over and he'd have bled out in three minutes. That brachial artery was this close." Mack pinched his thumb and forefinger together to illustrate, then put the vehicle in gear and headed to the road.

"You want to talk about what happened?" Gary asked her.

"No. I'm still trying to process it all." Emma held a hand to her forehead. "It's hard to think right now."

"When you're ready, you really should talk to someone you trust. You're in shock now but when it wears off, it will help to have someone to talk to about it."

CHAPTER 20

Adam appeared before the magistrate and explained the laundry list of proposed charges he had against Pablo Vasquez and Bill Ryan.

"This William Ryan is an FBI agent?" The magistrate looked at the paperwork, disbelief heavy in his expression.

"Yes, sir." Adam's entire body had begun to ache, his muscles and joints reminding him he was no spring chicken anymore.

"So, you set up a sting to nab a cartel assassin and ended up arresting an officer of the law." The magistrate typed a few things into his computer.

"William Ryan confessed to being involved in the distribution of the cartel's drugs and money. He's also a kidnapper and an attempted murderer. Not to mention the conspiracy to commit murder and accessory to murder charges for a fellow agent. Vasquez is willing to testify against him."

The magistrate just shook his head. "Pablo Vasquez,

now that's a name I've heard before. That man has so many warrants out on him. A real bad dude. He must be hoping for a deal if he offered to testify."

Adam agreed. "Won't do him much good though. With this count of murder and the attempted murder, he's probably going away for a very long time. We have the murder of the agent on video."

"I'd say this wasn't his lucky day then." The magistrate finished typing a few things, then waited for some papers to print that he handed to Adam. "Good job, Detective. You deserve a day off for this."

He waved the pile of papers. "Maybe after all the reports and paperwork are done. Have a good one."

Adam left the magistrate's office and headed to the public parking where he'd left his SUV. As he pulled open the door, he heard someone walk up behind him. Grabbing his gun off his hip, he spun around.

"Easy there, Adam. I come armed only with the word of God."

"Pastor Ben." He holstered his weapon. "I'm so sorry. It's been a rough day."

Pastor Ben held out his hand, and Adam shook it. It had been many years since he'd spoken to the pastor. "Good to see you, son. I may have heard a rumor or two. Is Emma Thomas going to be okay?"

"She is at the emergency room now getting some stitches. I'm headed that way to check on her."

"The whole town is already talking about the way you saved Emma and broke up the drug trafficking through Staunton.

You're quite the local hero now."

Adam shrugged. "It was good police work by a whole team from several different agencies."

Ben rested a hand on Adam's shoulder. "Teams need leaders, Adam. You've always been a good leader. I figured you'd lead our youth group one day. The entire church was saddened when you stopped attending."

Adam shifted his weight, uncomfortable with where the conversation was headed. "There were mitigating circumstances, as I am sure you remember."

"What happened that night was a tragedy. Miranda was a good girl but she definitely had a bit of a wild streak. She drove that car too fast even on good days. No one ever blamed you for that. Or for what happened to Leslie."

"I guess maybe I just blame myself enough for everyone."

All he wanted to do was get to Emma. "It's been great seeing you, Pastor, but if you don't mind, I really have to go."

Ben stepped away, and Adam closed the door. As he did, he heard the pastor say, "God bless you and keep you safe."

The unexpected conversation sat heavy on his mind as he drove to the hospital. He'd worked so hard for so long to lock away those memories and emotions and he just kept getting reminded of them over and over again. Heck, even Agent Ryan had known about Miranda's accident and Leslie's murder and tried to use both against him.

The lot nearest the emergency room was full, so Adam parked in the regular visitors' lot and walked through the hospital to where Emma was. When he reached the desk, the nurse sent him to curtain twelve.

Emma lay on the gurney, her eyes closed and a bright white bandage wrapped around her head. A tiny crimson stain had worked its way through the gauze. Her chin and cheek were bruised, and a smudge of dirt ran alongside her nose. She looked absolutely beautiful, and it took all of his self-control not to pick her up and carry her off into the sunset, like one of those romance book heroes.

Except the sun had set hours ago and he was no cowboy or prince or whatever. Just a cop in a small town who'd fallen in love a long time ago with the one girl he'd never be able to have. Now that the case was over and Emma was safe, she'd head back to Richmond the minute her parents returned to town.

"You just gonna stand there and stare at me like some creeper or come on in?" Emma peeked at him from under her long, thick lashes.

"I'm not a creeper." Adam walked in and pulled the curtain closed. "I just didn't want to disturb you if you were asleep."

"Not sleeping. Those fluorescent lights were making my eyes ache, so I closed them." Emma leaned up on an elbow. "I don't smell chimichangas."

Adam chuckled. "I didn't think I'd be able to smuggle them past the nurses. We'll head there as soon as they spring you from the joint."

"I've just been waiting on my ride." Emma winked and smiled.

"Sorry. The magistrate's office took longer than I thought."

The curtain slid open, and a nurse walked in wearing a pink scrub top with images from Cinderella all over it. "Well, you must be Ms. Emma's knight in shining armor come to take her back to the castle."

"I don't know about all that. I'm just here to give her a ride home in my police car."

"Oh! How romantic! You gonna run the blue lights and everything?" The nurse pressed one of her hands over her heart and fanned herself with the other.

Adam held his hands up in the air. "We're not a couple."

"No," Emma added quickly.

"If you two aren't destined to be together, then I'm Miss Cindy-rella waitin' on my prince." The nurse winked at Adam as she handed Emma a clipboard full of papers and a pen. "If you'll just sign here, you'll be free to go."

Emma signed and handed it all back to her. The nurse selected three sheets and folded them in half before handing them to Emma.

"Thank you," Emma said, accepting them.

"Take it easy and get plenty of rest, ya hear?" The nurse disappeared through the curtain before Emma could reply. Adam helped her down off the bed.

Keeping an arm around her shoulders, he walked her out of the hospital and to his truck.

"Where did you park? West Virginia?" Emma poked him in the ribs lightly with her elbow.

"Very funny." He pointed to the vehicle. "It's right there, silly girl."

Adam helped her into the passenger seat, resisting the

urge to kiss her right there in the parking lot. Instead, he closed the door, and jogged around to the driver side. Once he was settled in the seat, he pulled out the necklace he'd found on the ground and handed it to Emma. "I thought you might want this back."

Her eyes widened as she realized what he'd given to her. "Where did you find it?"

"On the ground near the old log. I can't believe you were wearing it."

"I never take it off." She smiled as she held it up. The smile quickly turned to a frown. "It's broken now though."

"Don't worry, we can get it fixed." He reached over and lightly squeezed her hand holding the necklace.

Emma reached in the back and grabbed the purse she'd left there that morning. Opening a small zipper pocket, she tucked it inside. "For safe keeping until then."

It took everything he had to not pull her into his arms right then and there. The realization of how close he'd come to losing Emma hit him hard in the gut.

He needed a distraction. Adam took his phone out of his other pocket and pulled up the number for his favorite Mexican restaurant.

"What do you want? I'm going to call in a take-out order."

"One of everything?" Emma's stomach let out a loud growl on cue. They both laughed.

"You got it." Adam dialed and gave a large order of all his and Emma's favorites. "There. That should satisfy us both." He ended the call and put the phone down on the console between them. "Want me to take you home?"

"My stuff is still at your uncle's cabin."

Adam turned the truck on, put it in gear, and pulled out of the parking lot. "I can bring it to you tomorrow afternoon. Or we can pick it up when we go get the dogs."

Emma nodded. "It might be nice to sleep in my own bed tonight."

"It's settled then." They drove to the restaurant in comfortable silence. Adam reached over and took her hand in his. Emma gave him a sideways glance but made no move to pull her hand away.

When they made it to the restaurant, Adam ran in and grabbed the food, then drove them the rest of the way to the Thomas house.

Emma sighed when he pulled into the driveway. "Home, sweet home. All these years away I never realized how much I've missed this house. And Staunton." She turned to look at him. "And you."

"I'm just glad you're here, for however long that is." Adam opened the door and stepped out of the truck, grabbing the food from the back seat. Emma was already out of the truck when he made it to her side.

She didn't say anything as she led him inside. Adam set the bag of food on the counter while Emma washed her hands. "I'm going to change real quick. These clothes make me feel grimy."

"No problem. I'll set the food out on the counter, and we can eat when you get back."

"Okay. Won't take me long."

She disappeared down the hall, and Adam started opening containers. Everything smelled so good, his stomach began to rumble. By the time Emma returned, his plate was loaded with a towering pile of Mexican food.

"Feel better?" Adam asked as she grabbed a plate and started to fill it.

"So much. The doctor said I can't shower until tomorrow so I'm going to have to deal with the dried blood and dirt in my hair though."

Adam set his plate down and walked over to where Emma stood. He took her plate and set it on the counter, then pulled her in close. "I really thought I'd lost you today."

Emma wrapped her arms around his waist and leaned into his chest. "I'm not that easy to get rid of."

"I'll miss you when you go back to Richmond." He kissed her forehead.

"Why do you keep saying that? Are you trying to get rid of me? After our talk last night, I thought…." She let the rest of the sentence go unsaid.

Adam pulled back and tilted her head up so he could look in her eyes. "I guess I just assumed when your parents returned, you'd get back to your life."

She shrugged. "Maybe. Or maybe I don't have anything in Richmond to go back to. Maybe I'm trying to start a new life."

"Here in Staunton?"

She shrugged again. "Why not? I mean, if I had a reason to stay…."

No longer able to resist, Adam leaned down and pressed

his lips to hers. The kiss was gentle and sweet and everything it should be for two people falling in love. "Would there be any particular reason you'd stay?"

Emma rose on tiptoe and pulled his mouth back to hers. "I'm not sure."

This kiss was full of promises and a future. She never wanted it to end. When they finally parted, Adam held her close. "I don't want you to leave here ever again."

"I don't want to leave." Emma ran her fingers over the soft material of his shirt. Her touch, gentle and sweet, gave him a glimpse of a future he knew he wanted.

He shook his head. "I don't either. It's time we faced the memories head-on, and I think we should do it together. Especially if we're going to spend our lives together."

Her green eyes widened. "Adam Marshall, if you just asked me to marry you—"

He reached for her again, but Emma stepped out of the way. "Come back here, Emma. Please. I wasn't proposing. Yet. When I do, you won't see it coming. But I want you to know that is the end game for me. You are it for me. I have loved you since the day we met. I've just been too hung up on my own issues to realize it. If I had, I'd have gone after you years ago and brought you back home where you belong."

She put her hands on her hips and tried to look annoyed, but Adam saw something else in her eyes. "And if I refused?"

"You wouldn't have."

"You're awfully confident, officer." She relaxed her stance, and he pulled her back in once more.

"Not confident, just hopeful." He kissed her gently. "I love you, Emma Thomas."

"I love you too, Adam Marshall. And yes, I'll marry you one day."

"That's all I needed to hear, future Mrs. Marshall."

When he kissed her that time, he felt their hearts become one. The woman he'd love since they were children loved him back and that was all he needed to know.

ACKNOWLEDGEMENTS

So many years ago, when I dreamed of becoming a published author, I found a tiny publisher in a newsletter accepting un-agented submissions. Knowing what I know now about my craft, it was sheer luck that my manuscript landed in the hands of my first ever editor. Thank you, Allie, for your vote of confidence back then and your continued friendship now. I wouldn't be where I am now without that opportunity.

I need to give a huge thank-you to author Samatha Harris and author Maria Vickers for holding my feet to the hypothetical fire with late night writing sprints and never-ending support. I never thought I'd get back on track after losing my mom.

My biggest thank-you goes to Hot Tree Publishing and Becky for taking on this project, my amazing editor Olivia for really making me work hard to get this story to amazing, and BookSmith Designs for the beautiful cover.

Finally, thank you and I love you to my husband Eric for always supporting my dreams.

ABOUT THE AUTHOR

Science teacher by day, writer and baseball mom by night, Carolyn LaRoche lives near the ocean with her husband, two boys, rescue puppy, and four cats. She loves crocheting, books, food videos and trying new recipes.

Stay connected with Carolyn.

FACEBOOK: /CarolynLaRocheAuthor/
TWITTER: @CarolynLaRoche
GOODREADS: /carolynlaroche
INSTAGRAM: @carolynlarocheauthor

ABOUT THE PUBLISHER

Hot Tree Publishing opened its doors in 2015 with an aspiration to bring quality fiction to the world of readers. With the initial focus on romance and a wide spread of romance subgenres, Hot Tree Publishing has since opened their first imprint, Tangled Tree Publishing, specializing in crime, mystery, suspense, and thriller.

Firmly seated in the industry as a leading editing provider to independent authors and small publishing houses, Hot Tree Publishing is the sister company to Hot Tree Editing, founded in 2012. Having established in-house editing and promotions, plus having a well-respected market presence, Hot Tree Publishing endeavors to be a leader in bringing quality stories to the world of readers.

Interested in discovering more amazing reads brought to you by Hot Tree Publishing? Head over to the website for information:

WWW.HOTTREEPUBLISHING.COM